From the author of
The Extraordinarily Ordinary Baker Street

Janice

A coming of age tale of hope and perseverance

AF084485

JEAN GOULBOURNE

LMH PUBLISHING LIMITED

© 2022 Jean Goulbourne
First Edition
10 9 8 7 6 5 4 3 2 1

All rights reserved. No part of this book may be reproduced, stored in a retrieval system, or transmitted, in any form or by any means, electronic, mechanical, photocopying, recording, or otherwise, without the prior written permission of the publishers or author.

This is a work of fiction. Names, characters, places and incidents either are the products of the author's imagination or are used fictitiously, and any resemblance to actual persons, living or dead, events or locales, is entirely coincidental.

All LMH Publishing Limited titles are available at special quantity discounts for bulk purchases for sales promotion, premiums, fund-raising, educational or institutional use.

Editor: K. Sean Harris
Cover Design: Roshane Mullings
Book Design, Layout & Typesetting: Roshane Mullings

Published by LMH Publishing Limited
Suite 10-11, Sagicor Industrial Park
7 Norman Road
Kingston C.S.O., Jamaica
Tel.: 876-938-0005; 876-938-0712
Fax: 876-759-8752
Email: lmhbookpublishing@cwjamaica.com
Website: www.lmhpublishing.com

Printed in the U.S.A.   ISBN: 978-976-657-072-9

CATALOGUING-IN-PUBLICATION DATA
AVAILABLE AT THE NATIONAL LIBRARY OF JAMAICA

Dedicated to
my niece Milena and my nephew Marc.

Chapter 1

Janice looked through the crack in the window. The windowpane was dirty. She looked over at the yard dotted with small houses. The yard was surrounded by a rotting zinc fence. In one corner stood the standpipe where Miss Clara was bathing. The water was running as usual. It never seemed to stop running even in times of severe drought in the city. Miss Clara was naked except for her panties, which hung about her like a balloon. As she washed herself, she sang a song. "When the roll is called up yonder, I will be there." She used the rag to wash underneath her pendulous breasts. Then she rinsed and wiped herself. Janice continued to look. Everybody knew what Miss Clara looked like.

Everybody knew how everybody else looked in the tenement yard. One person's business was everybody else's business in the tenement yard. Janice herself bathed like that under the standpipe and had done so for as long as she could remember.

All around the yard, the fowls scratched at the red earth, clucking as they scratched, their feathers as red as the dirt around them. The fowls had lice and all the children and adults in the yard tried to avoid them. They roosted under the floorboards of the houses and sometimes the lice broke through and bit the occupants in their beds, but the hens supplied the people there with eggs, and sometimes Miss Clara sold the eggs to the people in the corner shop and took home some well needed money.

In one corner of the yard, a baby boy played. He wore a dirty blue chemise but his naked buttocks were as red as the dirt in which he played. He had an old cotton reel in his hands and as he played with it, he smiled and laughed to himself. Close to him stood the coolie plum tree where all the children went when they came from school. The fruit from that coolie plum tree provided money for lunch for so many people in the yard. Now the fruit was almost ripe as it was January. When the fruit was ready, the boys took the little green, flecked with yellow, ripe plums and sold them on the streets downtown. Coolie plums ripened after Christmas and that was the time when they all needed money to get back to school and to provide food for the yard. It was the only tree that stood on that piece of ground. In fact, it was the only green plant that grew there because the earth was too hard, and the fowls and the playing children would not allow any other green thing to thrive, not even the grass that Janice's mother Rosemary had tried so often to grow.

Miss Clara stopped singing. She held up her head and called, "Charlie! But a weh that boy is sah? I tell him to look for the fowl egg them under the house. Every time I want him, him gone. Soon tu'n gunman pon me. On all a we. Trials and tribulations all the time." She resumed singing. "When the roll is called up yonder, when the roll is called up yonder."

Miss Clara put on her clean brown blouse, the one with the patch on the sleeve, and a gray skirt. Miss Clara almost always wore that skirt around the yard on a Saturday evening. It was as predictable as the Saturday evening chicken foot soup.

JANICE

She wiped her feet and pulled on her slippers which were made of a thick rubber. It meant that Miss Clara was almost ready to cook her chicken foot soup and go to her room to read her Bible. She was a very religious woman. All day Sunday Miss Clara spent in the church up the road and when the service was going on, the noise was unbearable as the pastor called for more testimonies, songs, prayers and money. Miss Clara usually wore white as she was in the choir. She sang alto and loved to boast about the time the pastor made her sing solo at convention. It was the most important day of her life so far and she longed to repeat the feat. Only that was four years ago and now she sang with the rest of the choir and was never called on to sing solo again.

"Charlie!" she shouted again. "I want the eggs for breakfast tomorrow morning you know. I don't have anything else but mint tea and crackers, and tomorrow is Sunday. We must make a little change for the Lord's day. Charlie! But is where him is sah? Heaven give holiday. That boy is a trial."

Miss Clara's hissed teeth could be heard all the way across the yard as she crossed the hardened dirt and went into her little one-room. She lived in the room with Charlie, her fourteen-year old grandson and his twelve-year old sister Shellie-Ann. Miss Clara's only child, Delroy, had left the children with her and had gone overseas from Shellie-Ann was a baby. She had heard nothing from him since. Miss Clara had never known the mother of her grandchildren. Rumour had it that she was in prison for running drugs. Nobody knew for sure. But Miss Clara lived in the hope that Delroy would write and even send a few US dollars for the children. It distressed her to know that after all she had done for Delroy, it had come to this. Shellie-Ann was spending the Saturday at a friend's house up the lane where she was studying for the GSAT examination. GSAT would be in two weeks time. Everyone was praying that she would be placed at a good high school, just as Janice had been placed by the old common entrance exams five years before.

Janice smiled as she watched Miss Clara. Miss Clara was like a grandmother to the whole tenement yard. Even Janice's mother, Rosemary, regarded her as such.

"She holds us together as a family," Rosemary often said.

As Janice looked up, she saw the gate open and Rosemary enter the yard. She looked tired but there was something about her that was different today. Janice looked at her expectantly. What was up? she wondered. Rosemary walked with a sure step, a more confident step than she had before.

Janice stood and opened the door. Rosemary entered, threw her parcels on the bed and hugged her daughter.

"Is what happen Mama?" asked Janice.

"We moving out of here."

"Moving? Where to? Mama what happen? You get a job?"

"To look after an old lady in Barbican. Rich people, and there is space for you to live there too. You can come and help me when you come home from school. Mr. Soares say him will give you pocket money so that you can go to school in the day and help me in the evenings. They have a room at the back where we can live."

Janice took in the news quietly. She stared at Rosemary. Her eyes filled with tears of joy.

"Mama, it was hard for you to go to school on Saturdays and do the practical nurse course after you work all week as a domestic helper. But it work out. How the pay?"

"Good enough, I only hope the old lady live long though. I want to see you go through with you high school and pass you CXC. Janice mi child. Things working out at last. No more rent to pay. I only hope that when you leave school and get a job, you can go a little further in your studies and then help me buy a house. I going to save money, Janice. You watch and see. At last. Thank you Jesus."

JANICE

Janice turned and looked at the room which she had called home practically all her life. She saw the rotting wooden floors, the one bed that her mother owned and in which they slept, the dresser with the figurines that her mother prized. She saw the small wardrobe that held all their clothes and the dinette set with the four chairs in one small corner of the room. The table was stacked with her books, pens and pencils. From the roof hung a lone light bulb from a cord and around a corner from the bed, stood a shoe stand with a few pairs of shoes, one pair each for school or work, and one each for church for her mother and herself. It was a small room and full of the familiar things that had grown around them over the years. They would leave all this behind and live in another place where most likely there would be no rats, no fowl lice creeping through the floorboards and no cockroaches to contend with.

Janice felt her heart bursting. Maybe she could take home a friend or two from her school to her new living quarters. It was something that she had never dared to do in all her five years at the exclusive school that she attended. Janice was bright, she was a scholarship winner and an achiever, but from the wrong side of town. She had tried never to expose her living conditions to the friends with whom she studied. She had never gone to their homes when they used to invite her in, because she feared that they would want her to invite them home to her own one-room in the tenement yard in the inner city community in eastern Kingston.

Janice thought now of her father. He was serving time in prison. He had been caught with an illegal gun and had been put in prison. That had been five years ago, just as Janice had been entering high school. She had never dared to tell her school friends, preferring instead to say that he had died in an accident. Janice was ashamed of her father. He had been a gunman and a burglar. It was her mother that Janice loved and it was she who had helped to make her what she was now. A good student in school, someone with leadership qualities and a senior prefect in fifth form. Usually it was sixth formers who were senior prefects, but Janice had excelled, throwing off her old self to adapt to the new life in the prosperous area with its money, its mansions and its vastly different attitude towards life and living. But she had not abandoned her mother and never would. Rosemary admitted to her daughter that Janice's father had been a mistake from the get-go, but love was strange. Rosemary had left the small farm in the deep countryside where her parents lived, to live in the city before Janice was born. She had found shelter in her aunt's house and had worked as a clerk in a downtown store. Then she had met Bert.

Bert had changed her life and she had gotten pregnant. Her aunt had put her out and her parents had been disappointed in her. Later, she had realized that the wealth Bert spoke so often of, came from stealing and house breaking. Life had never been the same again. Bert had got a gun and had got caught. It had seemed like the end of life for Rosemary until her daughter's birth. Janice had given her hope. Bert had been in and out of prison since then and now he was doing a very long stretch.

Janice was still thinking when she turned to her mother.

"Then Mama, what 'bout de furniture? What we going to do with them?"

"Maybe send them to country. Papa will put them up for us. I don't want to sell them as they were too hard to buy. Prices so high nowadays, I coulda never buy them back again."

"Mama, I going to save up the pocket money. Maybe start a bank account. I want it to help me through university. And later I will buy you a real nice house. Maybe in Cherry Gardens, or in the hills like Red Hills."

"Aye Jan Jan, we can only dream. We can only dream."

Rosemary set about preparing dinner. The inevitable chicken foot soup. Janice loved chicken foot soup. She loved eating the flesh off the bony chicken feet. She would take them out and lick them clean, then she would turn to the flour dumplings and the yam that was in the soup. Chicken foot soup was a must for everyone in the yard and if one family ran out of enough money, another family was there to help.

Suddenly, there was a howl from the yard. It was the baby who was sitting on the ground. Janice got out of her reverie and rushed outside.

"Junior what happen to you?" she asked as she ran. The year and a half old child was alone in the yard. Miss Clara who usually watched him, seemed to have left for a short while in search of her grandchild Charlie. He seemed to be hungry. Janice picked him up and crooned softly, kissing his dirty cheek in the process. Then she took him inside her own room and put him on the floor beside the bed. He wiped his eyes with his hands and smiled, knowing that food was on the way. It was always like this. Junior's mother, Simone, went downtown on Saturdays from early morning, hawking her goods on the city streets. She was a nineteen-year old girl who was trying to make it among the numerous vendors and street persons on the downtown streets. Sometimes she went farther afield to Falmouth or Mandeville by mini- bus, coming in late at nights to her child. The child's father had disappeared when he heard that she was pregnant. He had claimed that it was not his and he was not prepared to support any 'jacket'. She had borne her shame and had welcomed the child into her life after Miss Clara had taken her in and helped her. She too had been country bred and had known little of the ways of the city when she came to Kingston three years earlier. The victim of abuse from her own father and mother in the countryside, she had come to seek her fortune. Things had begun to pick up for her and she had some money in the bank. She also threw 'partner' with her friends and would try to put her 'draw' to good use when it came around. It was she, Simone, who helped out when the others were down financially like when someone got sick and had to see a doctor, or even go to the hospital or was short on the rent. Because of this, Junior was everyone's baby and although he often sat in the dirt in the yard, he had the love and care of everybody there.

The baby ate some crackers while Janice prepared some cornmeal porridge on the small oil stove.

"Going to bathe him and put him to bed Mama," she said as she mixed the porridge which was getting thick in the pot. "Simone not coming home for now."

"Right," answered her mother, "you do that while I peel the yams and fix up the vegetables for the soup."

There was a companionable silence in the room as the baby ate the porridge that Janice fed him while Rosemary got dinner ready. Then Janice got out the baby clothing that they kept for times like these and took the baby to the standpipe. Gently, she bathed him and dried him in a clean towel and put on his clothes. Then she took him inside, and hugged him. Soon the child was sleeping and the soup was bubbling on the fire. Not wanting to wake the child, mother and daughter sat quietly waiting for the soup to finish cooking. Both were thinking of the changes that were coming and what it would mean to their lives. Janice went once more to the window and looked through the crack in the window-pane. Life is full of change, she throught. What would this bring? What would leaving all this behind bring to her life?

Thoughts of school went through her mind. It was going to be so much easier for her now. She would be living in a better neighbourhood. She would be earning a little money to help her through school, and her mother was also going to be comfortable in a fairly well paying job. At least it would be better than the household helper's work of washing and ironing at several different people's houses that she used to do each week.

Janice thought of her best friend at school, Serena. But even though she was her best school friend, Serena had never visited her tenement yard or known the conditions under which she lived. True, she too lived in a less than sophisticated neighbourhood but Janice was certain that her house was not in a tenement yard, nor did she have to bathe under the standpipe in the open yard.

Janice thought too of her major arch rival at school. The one who had mocked her when she became senior prefect. Catalina Nathan was a wealthy uptown girl who swore that she was the queen of the crop and no one could upstage her. Catalina had been known to bring down just about anyone who attempted to do anything better than she could, and she had done everything to discredit Janice. She had even lied to some students and teachers about Janice, calling Janice a thief and a liar.

Janice had once won a prize for speech in the school's eisteddfodd and had beaten Catalina for the top award. That had been when she was in fourth form and Catalina was in fifth. Then to make things worse, Janice had been made a prefect, then a senior prefect. Catalina was livid.

Janice smiled as she remembered Catalina. She wondered if she, like Catalina, could visit uptown restaurants now or even go to a nightclub just once. Catalina was known to frequent nightclubs and to dress in clothes sold at boutiques. As the soup boiled and mellowed in the pot and the quiet snores of little Junior and her own mother's almost silent breathing cast an air of quiet and contented expectation over the room, Janice continued to dream. Maybe tomorrow was not too bad after all. Maybe things would really change for the better and maybe Catalina would not laugh at her, and maybe she could take her friends home sometimes and pretend that her mother was a fully qualified private nurse that had been trained overseas. But no, that would be lying though her mother was a nurse of sorts. She now had her certificate to prove it. Maybe her mother could also go on after this to be an enrolled nurse. Maybe she, Janice, could help her. Her thoughts went here and there as she remembered school and the challenges she had undergone and would still undergo. CXC exams were some months from now and later, she hoped she would go on to university to study pharmacology.

Suddenly, Rosemary jumped up.

"Soup ready," she said. "Wonder where Miss Clara gone sah? I want to tell her about me good fortune." She took the ladle. "Come Jan Jan," she said. "Drink you soup. We will have to plan. We have to get the furniture to the country to Papa and get ready to leave this place. Going to miss it though."

She added thoughtfully as she pushed a few stray strands of hair back from her face, "Going to miss everybody even little Junior here with him cotton reel. Well is so life go you know Jan Jan. Change and change. What my mama used to say? No progress without change. Like you bury the past and you slip into the new. Like getting a new dress and you burn the old one. Come. Soup look good man, even though is me make it. Let me leave some for Junior too. Him always like a little chicken soup. And him growing up, nuh true?"

"Yes Mama," said Janice as she dipped into the soup and found the toes of the chicken. She pulled them out and sucked away, enjoying the succulent flesh as it left the bones.

Chapter 2

The news went around like a swift breeze that sometimes came during the hurricane months of June to November: 'Miss Rosemary and her daughter were moving. Miss Rosemary get a full time job and they going to live in a rich people house'.

The boys who hung about on the streets and spent their whole lives taunting the young girls and singing lyrically when they got them in the family way, turned to Janice who had ignored them so far in spite of the taunts and the innuendos.

"So Janice, you goin' rich an' switch?"

"Cho man, Janice will help we now, nuh true Janice?"

"You get a job too Janice? Hope you will remember me."

"So Janice, you a go hold up you head like mi queen. Come back to mi chile. Mi will take care a you. Nuh fret. Tu'n doctor and mi wi married to you too."

"So Janice how about you give we a piece before you leave? It really sweet you know. Ask all the gal them. Ask you mother. How you think she get you? From airplane?"

And the laughter would rock the place like the noise from the sound system that seemed to go on like a curse in the area. The dancehall madness prevailed in this little club close to the tenement yard and it took all of her efforts to blot out the sound when the music, if it could be called that, haunted the place.

"Fire bun! Fire!" the DJs screamed and every child knew the words and the voices and the tunes.

The young men hated informers and sang the songs that reviled informers with relish, and some of the young girls loved the songs that called them beef and browning and a good piece of meat.

The croaking voices of so many who wanted to be a Bob Marley overnight or a more modern Beenie Man or Shaggy or Sean Paul, could be heard practicing on into the night behind zinc fences. And every man wanted to 'bus a tune' and live big with the ten fingers full of gold rings and the Rolex watch on the left hand, and the huge gold chain over the Nike T shirt, designer sneakers and the BMW to show his status. They had arrived, just from singing a few tunes. And then it was the babies from the many girlfriends, especially the brown skinned babies who would represent them and lift their status even higher.

"Lawd, give me strength," Rosemary would say with a groan, as she watched the potential drug pushers who tried to croak their ways into the recording studios. "Lawd, give me the strength and the energy to change this."

But she had lived there for a long time now and little had changed, except herself. She had grown instead to accept what she saw in spite of the pain, and her only remaining wish was to get her daughter out before she too fell victim to the system. It was a system that crippled. It was a system that enslaved. "And is who say slavery done?" she would often ask herself as she saw another little belly begin to grow and another potential grandmother as youthful

JANICE

as herself take the tamarind switch to the bottom that had offended her.

Those who tried those ways and did not succeed, tried the way of sports. Football and now basketball was the craze. Cricket was disappearing from the scene with the demise of the West Indies Cricket Team. The Collie Smiths had gone with them and now the Michael Jordans took over. Everybody knew Michael Jordan for practically everybody had access to a television set. This was the inner city but this was not back-a-wall. Back-a-wall had gone with the sixties. And those who still could not put a set in their houses went to the shop on the street corner to watch TV, and knew the latest moves of the current stars and basketball heroes to boot. Everybody knew man and woman story, and everybody knew the news. Not just Jamaican news which was full of killing and death and the forever ecomonic crisis, but the international news too about places like Afghanistan and Syria even though few could identify those countries on a map, let alone know what a map looked like. The atlases were stored in the cupboards at the local schools and nobody in their homes had access to, or interest in them. The closest anyone came to understanding a map was to see the weather after the news and to wonder if the latest storm or hurricane was approaching.

"Yes man," said Charlie to Janice. "Mi proud of you. Hope you don't forget me you know. You is my role model though you never did know that. I want mi little sister to be like you even though I feel like I born to dead like most people down here, I want mi little sister to be just like you."

A short time after that encounter with Charlie, Janice walked up the road to the local post office, wondering how she was going to live far away from this world which was almost all she had ever known. She walked past the zinc fences and the dirt tracks, the many bars and numerous churches of so many denominations in which people like herself, Miss Clara and Rosemary would worship in on Sundays. She walked past the fish vendors who sat in front of their wares with open legs guarding the fish in front of them, and past those who sold coconuts from their carts and shouted out, "Drink di water fe wash off you heart! It good for your daughter, it good for you and it good for the father!" Further down the road were the tin stoves on which jerk chicken and jerk pork were cooked on Friday evenings and many a home would depend on that for the Friday evening fare.

    She walked past the hut where Maas Simpleman as they called the tailor, sewed the occasional pair of pants for whoever could afford a new one; past the vendors selling coal for those who had not yet bought an oil stove or a gas stove for their kitchens; past the local grocery shop with the rum bar where the men and some women got drowned in liquor and slept off Saturday nights in a stupor as though to forget the latest woes or celebrate the latest victory; past the lottery shop and the race horse betting shop where the men and women lined up in droves to buy a horse or catch a lucky break with ready money for the next week. Then she went past the local school gates shuttered and protected from the gunmen who were likely to invade if one person got out of line, down to the yard where the local reggae band practiced, and finally into the general square where people sat around and cursed the government, their history and the neighbour for their woes and rejoiced when a child passed the exams to go to a school uptown. On that child's shoulders, the future of the family rested. As she walked, she heard the noises of the inner city, saw the joys and pain of the inhabitants, and wondered how she would live outside of what was familiar and part of her system, and move beyond this world that held a vast portion of her soul.

But she would go. Just as she had left the school in the inner city five years ago and enrolled somewhere that was vastly different from anything she had ever known. The uptown Catholic school with its strict rules, the students speaking perfect English and its attendant wealth, had been far removed from her psyche. It had been hard to settle in, but she had settled in with the help of teachers, her mother and the world of books that she had for so long loved. She was now on the way to the exams that meant so much to her. The CXC exams which would mean the College of Technology if she was to succeed in them.

As she walked down the road, she saw the tiny building in a corner of the square, the local library, a place where she had spent countless hours learning the business of books and building a mind that was full and growing even fuller with the need to learn more. She paused and decided to go in. She needed to tell Miss Hillman, the librarian, of the move she was about to make. Miss Hillman had seen her need to learn and had nurtured that need, getting more books just for Janice and for the few others in the area that were serious about learning.

She walked past the small patch of grass littered with periwinkle blossoms that formed some sort of a garden in front of the one-room with the bathroom and tiny kitchen at the back of the building. Janice entered through the open door and saw Miss Hillman. She was sitting at the desk piled with books, her graying hair surrounding a deeply lined face. Janice had known Miss Hillman for as long as she could remember the library. Miss Hillman looked up.

"Oh, Janice! I heard the good news already."

"Miss, I came to let you know. Can't believe you know already!"

"News flies faster than a crow in this place. Your mother stepped in just the other day. She wanted to tell me thanks for helping her with books for her course, and also for getting you hooked on books instead of drugs."

"Yes Miss Hillman. I come to say thanks too, and to say goodbye. I moving soon. We going to carry the furniture to the country first, then we going up there to live," said Janice.

"Good. I will miss you to no end, but life is full of changes. You know is like the water in a vase. If you don't change it, it will get stagnant and breed mosquitoes. I wish you well, Janice. I only hope you will not forget your roots and will come back around."

"I want to study chemistry and really learn about pharmacy. Miss Hillman you think I can do it? I want to change so many things."

"You can do anything you set your mind to Janice. Anything. Just work like a Trojan to get it and you will. Don't forget your roots. Without that you will be on sinking sand. Just remember what I've told you. You hear me?"

"Yes Miss Hillman. I hear you. I hear you loud and clear."

When Janice left the library that afternoon, she brushed tears from her eyes. Miss Hillman was so old now, she wondered if she would ever see or hear of her again.

On her way up she saw Brother Jonas. Brother Jonas had sold newspapers all his long life. Now he sat by the side of the road with the evening paper in his hands. He had already sold off his lot of newspapers and he had what was left for himself in his hands. He was reading silently. It was often said that Brother Jonas had taught himself to read, having never officially been to school in his childhood. He had attended JAMAL, which was a government reading programme for adults in the 1970s and had done well, Janice had heard the older people say, and it was to Brother Jonas that everyone turned to know what was going on. When the radio stations did not bring out the full reports or the TV stations had failed to let them know all the news, Brother Jonas was the spokesman. He spoke perfect English, had read voraciously and it was said, could even quote Shakespeare. His favourite memory gem was 'if you can't get what you love, love what you have' and Brother Jonas had done just that, taking care of his five children and his wife with the few hundred dollars he made each week, going to the library during the days and even buying a few books for himself.

Brother Jonas knew the value of education and all his children had done well. Why was Brother Jonas still living in the inner city among the gunmen and the cocaine addicts and the ganja smokers? Because it was where he had always lived and where he felt he was doing something of worth. He gave the news to the people around him and even assisted some of the younger boys and girls to learn to read.

His children had all got married and lived in middle class areas in the city and overseas, and they often came to see their mother and father still living in the conditions under which they all grew up. But they could not persuade their parents to leave. Mama Jonas cooked for many of the street children and provided them with pencils and paper from her own pocket. Mama Jonas sometimes sold in the fish market, getting up at daybreak to get the fish by the side of the pier downtown, and then going to Coronation Market to sell her wares. She was famous for her sprat fish that was fried so crisp you could even eat the bones.

Brother Jonas looked up as Janice walked by.

"Yes, my child. I heard the news," he said quietly. "Take every opportunity that comes your way. Don't blow it you hear me? I have never lived anywhere else but trials are not just here in this place I call home. Trials are everywhere. More uptown people commit suicide than the starving ones here in the inner city. Remember this, when you have too much, you will have little to live for. And if you have too much, remember to give. Give till it hurts. But I wish you well. And your mother too. Don't forget your father in prison. He is a human being just like yourself. You are of his seed. Don't forget that. You might not remember Old Jonas when you move out of here. But I will remember you. And I hope I will read good news about you in the newspapers one day. Good news, you hear me girl? Good news."

"Yes, Brother Jonas. Yes, I hear you. I hope I won't disappoint you. And I can't forget you Brother Jonas. You are the most positive person that I know."

"You say so now. But when the big life take you, you will forget. I am an old man now. I wouldn't mind if you come to mi funeral. But I will forgive you if you don't. I gone seventy-six years now. And that is a long life to live in a place where the guns bark daily and hunger stalk the land like a smelly evil wind."

Janice looked at him, an icon in the community and she felt the pull of tears. She brushed them aside and walked away from him as he turned back to the evening paper, wet his fingers and turned the page.

She went to the post office, got no mail and then walked up the road through the myriad of streets and tracks to her home in the tenement yard. Miss Clara was bathing Junior under the standpipe. She looked up as Janice entered the yard.

"Is you Janice," she said, "you see Charlie? I can't find that boy at all. Everyday is the same thing. Charlie gone like lightning after rain. Trouble and tribulations and crosses on the land in mi old age. But I glad for you and you mother. I truly glad for you and you mother. Just don't forget us, you hear me?"

Janice was almost choking with emotion now.

"Miss Clara, thanks. No I don't see Charlie. Him must be somewhere down the road. I don't know."

She stumbled into the room and fell onto the bed. The tears flowed and the sobs were deep in her throat.

So many kind people, so many people dying here never leaving here and growing here just to die. What can I do? How can I leave all this behind? How can I?

JANICE

Janice slept and forgot that her mother had asked her to cook the evening meal.

It was late evening when she woke and found her mother around the oil-stove cooking callaloo and rice and peas.

Chapter 3

That Friday evening after school, Janice and Rosemary packed up their furniture and other belongings, and headed off for the countryside. They were going to south St Elizabeth where Rosemary's parents lived and where she had grown up. They had to take the furniture there to be stored in one of the rooms that Rosemary's father had allotted for storage. She looked forward to the trip to her grandparents' home. They were farmers and were embedded in the area known as the breadbasket of Jamaica. They did fairly well on their five acres and Rosemary often said to Janice that she wondered why she did not just go home to help her aging mother and father on the farm. But although things had changed since her teenage years and there were now many opportunities for Janice for schooling, Rosemary could not go back to the situation of her father telling her what to do. She had been away too long and her brother and his wife now helped to take care of things. They had their own little house right there on the five-acre plot.

JANICE

The moving van drove out of the tenement yard and onto the roadway past the zinc fences and the entrance to the many lanes, down to Washington Boulevard and unto the highway and they were away like a breeze. Janice sat in the back of the van with a young man who would lift the furniture, while her mother sat up front with the driver. The back was open and soon the breeze began to cool the heat that had enveloped them all, and Janice enjoyed the ride, hoping all the time that it would not rain.

They drove past the canefields, past Ferry Station where the famous cotton tree on which slaves were hanged once stood, and the road was as crowded as the city but the cars were speeding on the highway. The van sped along as well. They passed the St. Catherine and Clarendon plains and then they were close to the hills of Manchester and climbing. It got noticeably cooler, in fact almost cold and they bypassed the town of Mandeville and headed down Spur Tree Hill to hit the St Elizabeth plains, and the heat enveloped them again. They were headed for Bull Savannah where people made money from farming and where most of Rosemary's family lived.

The terrain had changed with each parish and Janice often wondered at the infinite variety that made Jamaica such an interesting little island. As they entered the parish of St Elizabeth, one could see the fields of thyme, escallion and tomato, and around the plants were the dried guinea grass that kept in the moisture. South St. Elizabeth was known for its times of drought and the people, hardy and hardworking folks, had devised their own way of dealing with the persistent lack of rain. The faces of the people too, were different. Many were fair skinned with curly hair and were obviously of German descent; many had come from Germany after slavery. Janice knew all this from her history lessons at school.

Soon they were nearing Bull Savannah. The two and a half hour journey had seemed to speed along fast and they were now at the house of her grandparents who were waiting to greet them.

Even the speech was different. The St. Elizabeth drawl they called it, and soon Janice was in the arms of her grandmother and grandfather. They were to spend the night there and get back to the tenement yard tomorrow, Saturday morning, so that Rosemary could begin work on Monday.

Maas Jack was glad for his daughter and so was Miss Nellie, his mother. Janice's Uncle John came and gave Rosemary a hearty slap on the back.

"Glad fi you," he said. "Things a gwaan fi you at last. Eh Rosie?"

Janice's little cousins gathered round and they all sat in the hall and had a good little chat before Miss Nellie brought out the jerk pork and bammies that she had prepared for them. It was a feast.

After that, they explored the fields and John showed them the new fruit trees that he had planted. He had invested heavily in papaya saying that he had a good market now, and later he would plant broccoli, a fairly new vegetable.

It was a tired Janice who slipped between the covers of the sweet smelling bed of starched white sheets and covers, and slept that night. The van had returned to Kingston without them and they had to get back to the city on the minibus. It meant taking a route taxi to Junction and then boarding a bus to the city.

They left the quiet countryside that morning to the encouraging smiles of Maas Jack, Miss Nellie and Uncle John and his wife and children, and soon they were on their way back to the heat and bustle of Kingston. The journey was long and the music disturbing. Janice was happy to leave the hot minibus even if it meant going back to the tenement yard. But that was for only one more night.

JANICE

That Saturday night, the entire group of people in the tenement yard came together to wish them well and to give them a send off. Miss Jenny made toto cake and the jerk chicken man down the road sold off a whole pan full of jerk chicken to the people in the yard. They bought beer for the men and bottles of Red Label wine and that had been topped off by a small band of mento singing men, who had come to play the old time music and 'hurt up' everybody's soul with the sweet mento that was like part of the spirit of the place.

Next day, tired and weary from the late night, they journeyed to the house that was now their new home. Janice saw the back room that she and her mother would share. There was a bedroom with a bathroom. There was a cook and a gardener for the family, and they also lived in separate rooms at the back. Janice's mother was to be nurse to the ailing old lady who had ruled the place with an iron fist before she took ill with cancer. At least so the gardener had told Janice. "Miss Iris was old iron," he had said. "She just a little rusty now but watch out, she hard to break."

She was Mr. Soares' mother. The children's mother had been unfaithful to her son and had left for overseas and never called again, leaving the two children, James and Cornelia, without a mother.

Miss Iris was holding court in a wheelchair. She had a head of scanty white hair and a deeply lined face that was once beautiful. She demanded a manicure every two weeks and insisted on a pedicure every month. She made sure that Rosemary knew that she had to call in the cosmetologist every week. She needed a shampoo every day and a bath every morning at ten o'clock.

Her room was to be kept clean and her bed linen immaculate. She wanted nothing less. She and her son were paying for this and paying well above the minimum wage.

Rosemary had to be there until Janice came in the evenings. Then Rosemary could go and rest a while. She was paying Rosemary extra on weekends and therefore she had to work, but she would give her one weekend off per month. She could do anything she liked then. Maybe Miss Iris would go to the country to be on the beach with Mr. Soares on that weekend. They had a beach house and the children liked to go there at least once a month for a break from this 'hell of a city'.

Janice looked at the blooming bougainvillea trees that hung over the immaculately white washed walls, at the oleander that framed the pathway to the house, at the mango and plum trees, and at the water that ran over the fountain like a tiny lake in the middle of the well-kept lawn. She listened to the silence that surrounded her, silence except for the honk of the occasional car horn, and wondered where the 'hell' was. She could not find it anywhere. Wealth oozed through the tufts of grass around every flower-bearing plant, and inside the main house, wealth devoured everything from the clean cream-coloured walls to the sheer curtains and the white living room furniture flecked with gold. The bedroom was decorated with curtains whose trellises Janice had never seen except in the occasional magazine in the library at school. The dining room had a long table and above the table hung a chandelier. Janice had never seen a chandelier other than in books.

And talk about books. There was a library. Janice wondered if she would ever be able to sit there in the armchairs and read and read. She remembered Miss Hillman and wondered how she would react to a library like this one. Janice remembered her literature classes at school. She remembered how Miss Hillman had taught her to love and appreciate books. Literature was now one of her favourite subjects. She hoped that Mr. Soares would not mind her borrowing books to read now and again, even if he did not like her sitting in his armchair like a guest in his house.

Mr. Soares was not there that weekend. He and the two children had gone to the beach house and had left Miss Iris to meet the new nurse and give all the instructions. Janice wondered about the children. Would they tease her? Would they be her friends? Would they be too stuck up and proud to even regard her? She wondered about their ages. How old was Cornelia? And was James still a boy? Today was a Sunday and they would be back late in the day to go to school on Monday morning. Which school did they go to? What did they look like? Janice longed to know. She would know later when they returned. She did not want to question the gardener too much and the cook seemed busy as she did not just cook, but cleaned and dusted the house as well.

For the rest of the day, Janice ironed her uniforms and unpacked the rest of their clothes. Her clothes looked pathetic against the splendor of her surroundings. She hung the clothes in the closet and the towels, underwear and t-shirts in the dresser drawers provided. She tested the bathroom and realized that her mother and herself had their own shower in their own private bathroom. Luxury untold, that was what it was.

Meanwhile, Rosemary busied herself at her job. Lifting and putting Miss Iris in bed whenever she wanted to rest. Sitting and talking to Miss Iris whenever she needed a talking companion, and even reading to her from a small devotional book that Miss Iris treasured. Miss Iris wanted to know everything about them. After all, they were her new companions and she had to know who she had brought into her house. Rosemary told her everything except the story of Janice's father. He was dead, she told Miss Iris. He had died from a sickness many years ago. Miss Iris looked as though she was satisfied with that explanation. It seemed that in spite of the iron will that Miss Iris was noted for, she had a very soft side. She seemed to like Janice and was happy that she attended a good school and was going to do CXC exams soon. She asked if she had already paid her exam fees and when told no but they were soon due now, she offered to ask her son to help with the fees.

Rosemary breathed a sigh of relief. She had been wondering where the money was going to come from and whether she would have to ask for a loan from the credit union into which she put a small sum of money whenever she could. It was the credit union that had helped her to buy her furniture in the past.

"Mama. I going to like it here," said Janice as they lay in bed that night.

"I think so. I think so to mi chile. The work will not be easy but then life never easy yet. Miss Iris not bad. She have a good heart."

"And the house so nice. And the cook can cook good Mama. Almost as good as you."

"One thing though, if you want chicken foot soup you better cook it yuh self," cautioned Rosemary.

"Yes Mama I know. Them things is for downtown people, not for the likes of them up here."

"I miss the old room though. Even the chicken lice," said Rosemary wistfully.

"Me too. And Junior and Miss Jenny and Charlie and Simone and everybody in the lane," said Janice.

"Anyway go to sleep. Is a hard day tomorrow. Night."

"Me too. Have to finish mi homework and help you with Miss Iris. Wonder what the children look like?" said Janice. But Rosemary was already deep in sleep. With a sigh, Janice rolled over. She would see the children in the morning as they were coming in late tonight. She slept.

Janice woke with a start. It was still dark outside. Rosemary was not beside her. She wondered where her mother had gone and why she was alone in this big room without the rotting floorboards and the dirty windowpanes. Then she remembered with a sigh as she rolled over, ready to go to sleep again. She now lived in a luxurious house. Her mother was now a private nurse to a wealthy old lady and she, Janice, was moving up. Up from the lane to this place that she had always longed to go. To a place where her friends at school could come and see her. As she lay there that morning, she remembered the library in the house and how she hoped that her friends from school could come and look at the books if they were reference books. She was determined to do well at her CXC exams and determined too to see the back of the lane even though she still missed the standpipe and bathing Junior, and Miss Clara bathing half-naked with her voluminous panties billowing around her as she scrubbed under her huge long breasts.

No more standpipe. Instead there was a private bath and she decided that she would buy body lotion and talcum powder to enhance the beauty of the bath. Janice stretched her hands above her head and sighed, and she put her head back on her pillow for a while.

"Bliss, sheer bliss," she said as she wiped a happy tear from her eyes.

"Janice." It was her mother, calling her.

"Yes Mama?" Janice was out of bed in a flash.

"You still sleeping? Come help me wash these few pieces of clothes. Miss Iris underwear. She say we can use the washing machine when is more clothes to wash than this. But since is just these few, just wash them in the wash room and rinse them out. The clothes line is right over there so at the back. The clothes pin in the big box under the wash table. Do it for me and breakfast soon ready. Miss Merline soon call you for yours. We will eat in the kitchen like yesterday."

Janice remembered. She was still a servant. So was her mother. She hurried to do her mother's bidding and was putting the underwear on the clothesline when Miss Merline the cook, called her and the gardener.

"Oonuh come eat. How you like you tea? Sweet sweet with nuff milk? Is saltfish and ackee today. With roast breadfruit. Come Rosemary. Miss Iris all right? She resting? Good. Come take you tea. Simon get another chair. Take the one from the out house. Is four of us now. Not me and you one any more. Well well. How oonuh sleep last night? Oonuh sleep real good?"

Janice sat and dug deep into a dish of saltfish and ackee.

"Yes Miss Merline," she said between mouthfuls. "I forget where I was. I did frighten when I wake up. But I am alright now. School today. I need to know where to take the bus and so on."

"Which school you go to?" asked Simon, the gardener.

Janice told him.

"Mmhm. You is bright, man. Only bright pickney go to that school."

Janice glowed a bit with pride and then asked, "How I get there by bus?"

"It better to take a route taxi from here. The bus them only pass far away down the road. The route taxis for upper Barbican will get you there in minutes and they don't charge you much more than the buses them. Just go out the gate and flag down the red plate taxis them that mark upper Barbican."

The four ate together like they had known each other for a very long time.

Later Janice boarded the route taxi down the road and headed off to school. She had still not met the children. Mr. Soares had apparently been held up and had come in very late the night before.

JANICE

It was not long before she arrived at the school gate and saw the masses of uniformed children and young people. It was an all girls school, a Catholic institution. She was not late but knew that the bell would soon go for devotions, and that she had to put away her schoolbag in her classroom and make her way to the hall. And as senior prefect, she made her way to the prefects' notice board to see if she was on the duty list for the week. She was. She had to take the first formers to devotion that morning and make sure that there were no stragglers and no latecomers.

As she made her way to the first form block, a few of her friends greeted her.

"Hi Janice," called Serena who was on her way to the bathroom.

"Hi there Serena," replied Janice. Her voice was light and cheerful, so cheerful that Serena called to her again.

"You in love or something?" she asked.

"Oh Lord no. Just happy."

"Excellent," said Serena, still a little puzzled. It was not as though happiness in Janice was strange, it was just that she looked not just happy, but exuberant.

Janice grinned and entered the first form block just as the bell for devotion rang.

"Come, come on! Put your bags away!" she shouted as the students moved towards the desks and then lined up for devotion. Hers was the voice of authority. She sounded like a teacher. One girl made a face and tried to make for the door to go to the bathroom.

"Come on, Sara," said Janice, as she grabbed her by the arm. "Not this morning again. Your hair is already combed. Devotion time now."

Sara mumbled something angrily and joined the queue. She had no wish to get another detention. Janice was too strict with them. The queue of girls, dressed alike, neat and well groomed, walked towards the hall and took their places in front of the hall right under the eyes of Sister Mary Gloria, the principal of the school. The rest of the school population joined them and they had devotion after which Sister Mary Gloria gave her usual pep talk with a few warnings and admonitions. The girls fidgeted as they were used to the usual Monday morning speeches. Then they filed out line by line to get back to the classrooms and to begin the day's work.

"What's up with Janice?" Catalina Nathan said to Serena as they watched Janice walk up the corridor with a song on her lips.

"Don't know, ask her," Serena replied with a giggle.

Catalina hissed her teeth and stalked off to the classroom on the sixth form block. She would find out. Maybe Janice had won the lottery or something like that. Something was up, a boyfriend at long last? The promise of an overseas trip after exams? Catalina had her own way of finding things out. Janice was too big for her boots, she needed to be taken down a peg or two. She, Catalina Nathan, would see to that.

The day passed relatively incident free and Janice went to the library in between classes and studied hard. She had her usual lunch of a beef patty and a drink, but she was not as hungry as she usually was at lunchtime, thanks to the big breakfast she had eaten that morning. At the end of the school day at two o'clock, she made her way home and her brain was still suffused with the song, 'Good Things Come to Those Who Wait'. She noted that she had to attend a prefects' meeting the following day and that there was more homework to complete that night. She flagged down a route taxi marked upper Barbican and did not see the smirk on Catalina's face as she watched her take the taxi that was clearly marked with the destination Barbican. So she has moved, Catalina noted. Maybe her mother had won the lottery. She would find out.

JANICE

Janice looked forward to seeing the children of the house. She knew that Cornelia attended a private school uptown and that James was still in a prep school also uptown, in fact, close to where they lived. That explained why there had been no rush to get them out that morning. Mr. Soares would drive them there in no time at all.

Simon greeted her at the gate. He opened it to let her through. She smiled at him. He grinned back at her.

"How things Janice?" he asked.

"All right," she said lightheartedly.

"Good man, maybe me and you can go out one day. You looking happy man."

"Listen Simon..." said Janice with a threat in her voice.

"Aww come on. You think you better than me?"

"Simon, I have to help mi mother with Miss Iris."

"Ah right, ah right," said Simon. He took the garden fork and began digging a hole in the ground. He dug ferociously.

Janice entered the room at the back of the house and dropped her bags on the bed. She had to watch that one there Simon. He was just a little uppish. After all she attended a high school. She had ambition. What did he expect of her?

Janice changed out of her uniform. She would have to get something better than this. The yard dress was threadbare. She had wanted to meet the children in something much better than this. A pair of shorts perhaps? With a nice blouse, or even a pair of old jeans cut in a sexy way. She would see about that when she got her first month's pay.

She found Rosemary with Miss Iris. Miss Iris greeted her with a smile.

"So you are home Janice!" she said. Her voice was low and her face was still a little twisted from the pain.

"Yes, Miss," said Janice. "What you want me to do, Miss?" she continued after smiling at Rosemary, as her way of greeting her mother.

"Just sit with me while your mother gets a little rest my dear. A half an hour or so till I get a little nap, then you can go and do your homework. All right Rosemary. Get some rest. Janice will take over."

Janice sat and chatted with the old lady. They spoke of school days. Miss Iris it seemed, came from a wealthy old family and had attended a boarding school in the countryside many years ago. She asked Janice what she was doing in CXC and what she wanted to become. When Janice told her that she wanted to be a pharmacist, she was thrilled.

"Good," she said. "We need people like those and the pay is very good these days."

She told Janice about her own profession. She had been a florist. She had owned her own flower shop in the city and she loved gardening.

"That explains why the place so beautiful," Janice said to her.

"And Simon does such a good job. He is a gem of a gardener and yet so young," Miss Iris replied. "I hope that he stays on."

By the time she had helped to lift the frail old lady onto her bed, the children came in to say hello to their grandmother.

Cornelia and James stood and stared at her for a long moment. Janice stared back. She had thought that Cornelia was much younger but she was about fourteen, just two years or so younger than Janice. She was slim with a pretty face and big brown eyes. Her hair was straightened and brownish as though she had coloured it brown. James was short and stocky. It was he who broke the silence.

"Hi there! Are you Janice, the new nurse's daughter?" he asked.

"Yes," answered Janice.

He came and shook her hand.

"Welcome," he said kindly.

"Thank you!" answered Janice with some surprise.

Cornelia snickered.

"Don't mind him," she said. "He is still a baby."

"I am not!" said James.

"Yes you are," said Cornelia. "James is just a baby," she sang.

"You are at it again kids?" A man of about forty something came through the door.

"Oh Janice," he said. "I am Mr. Soares. My mother told me all about you. You seem to have hit it off with her."

"Hello Mr. Soares," said Janice, smiling.

"How you doing? Liking it here?"

"Yes sir. Very much."

"Good. Hope we will all get on well together. Cornelia, James, get a bath and get to the books. Janice, my mother seems to want to sleep now. Maybe you had better hit the books yourself. You have exams in a few months time your mother was telling me."

"Yes sir!"

"So go study. And by the way, you may borrow my books in the library if you need them. Only return them, ok?"

"Yes sir. Thank you sir!"

It was a joyful Janice that went into her room and tackled the books that night and for many other nights that followed.

The week went away like ice melting in the sun. It was as if living in these new surroundings caused the problems of the past to seem almost non-existent; as though the past had never been; as though the tenement yards of downtown did not exist; as though Maas Jonas was somewhere on the planet but that she had never really known him; as though the boys who sat like restless lizards on the corner and jeered at her were in another country; as though Miss Hillman was real but had died way back when, when she, Janice, was a child; as though the zinc fences were somewhere in the universe but had never been a part of her own personal world. Janice seemed even to forget Miss Clara and was really angry when Rosemary suggested that they visit the tenement yard and see how everyone was one day when it was her weekend off. Janice's mother looked at her daughter and saw what so many others in the inner city saw in situations like these: *she get rich an' switch*. It had been happening all throughout history. A denial of self, a denial of past, a denial of friendships that had sustained in times of hardships and woe.

Janice turned her attention to another need. Clothes and shoes. She swore that she did not really have enough, she had to look good. She felt strange in those old 'ghetto clothes'. Those few dresses that had been bought in cheap stores downtown. Some had been bought from the street vendors. She needed a few from the uptown stores, real clothes like Catalina's. Real shoes like Miss Iris's. Rosemary began to despair. Had she done the right thing? Taken her daughter from what had become her real roots into the plastic world of the rich? Did Janice not see that they could not maintain the lifestyle of the Soares' family on the wages of a practical nurse?

But Janice went even further. They needed a house of their own so that they could buy their furniture at an uptown furniture store and fix it up really nicely like this one, with a garden and everything. She wanted it all and as fast as possible. Maybe even a swimming pool and a gardener to tend to everything.

For weeks Janice dreamed. For weeks Rosemary despaired. She knew the signs of trying to get into the fast lane without the means to sustain it. She wanted to curb Janice's wishes without hurting her. But how could she do it? Rosemary remained silent, hoping that time would cure all. She saw that Miss Iris could see the problems too but she said nothing. Time would tell.

Janice worked hard at preparing for her exams. Mr. Soares helped to pay her fees. Her mother had borrowed to pay the rest by asking for some of her wages in advance. Janice was given a little pocket money for helping her mother and the rest of the family out, so each week she saved in a new bank account and with the rest, she tried to save towards new clothes. Her lunch money and taxi fares also came from the allowance.

The weeks passed swiftly. Janice scarcely saw the children. They were either inside their rooms or at the dining table, or in the family room watching cable television. In the mornings, they left early for school and Janice had so much to do on her return home, including ironing their uniforms, that she scarcely had time to talk to them let alone become their friend. Mr. Soares was hardly home. It was Miss Iris that Janice saw most and she was so laced with the feeling of her own aristocracy and inherent superiority that even though she had a kind heart, Janice was a little afraid to be with her. Miss Iris reminded her too much of the slum she had come from because of the vast difference between her life and Janice's past life, and Janice felt that it was time to forget the past, put it behind her and move on to better and greater things.

Miss Merline was fine and Simon too. Miss Merline was proud to see her attending St. Eustace's and being a senior prefect and all. One day, Miss Merline asked her to help in the kitchen with the preparation of the salad and they got to chatting about school and what it was like.

"So how school today?" asked Miss Merline.

"School alright, is just that girl Catalina Nathan. She hate mi guts cause I always beat her at speech in eisteddfod. She say that somebody like me shouldn't know so much English and shouldn't speak like she." Janice hissed her teeth as she turned to face Miss Merline. "She too feisty and renk. Like is she one and people like she who should know English. I tell her I good on the patois but I good on the English too. Poor thing, she coulda never do a good Louise Bennett poem. I can do both Shakespeare and Louise Bennett and it hurt her no end."

"What you say she name?"

"Catalina Nathan."

"Catalina...not the Nathan them that come here sometimes and go up to the beach house now and again?"

"You know Catalina?"

"They live in Cherry Gardens. Her father have a big house there. Her brother race cars down on the Dover racetrack. Them have a business. Sell cars and car parts," said Miss Merline.

Janice turned to look at Miss Merline in dismay. If Catalina ever found out that her mother was a practical nurse and lived like a helper, her life at school would be torment. She would never let her forget it.

Janice had a new worry on her hands now. How to avoid Catalina. How to hide who she really was from her arch enemy. But it was not long before the real problem hit her hard like a cricket ball in the stomach. Mr. Soares was planning a little get together with his friends. He had completed a big business deal and was really anxious to let his friends know of his success. There was going to be drinks and a few games, including dominoes. Then maybe dinner after the general chatter and backslapping. Would Janice help Miss Merline to serve? Of course Janice had to say yes. Would she wear an apron please and a nice little dress to suit the occasion? Of course Janice had to say yes again. There could be no excuse. Mr. Soares had already paid part of her examination fees.

Janice dressed well that evening. She put on a new dress and a pair of black high heeled shoes.

But not too high in case she slipped with the trays in her hands. Then she put on the dreaded apron over her dress and combed her hair in her customary canerows. She looked at herself in the mirror. She looked like a real maid of an upper class family in the suburbs of London. She hated herself.

That evening the guests turned up in semi-formal outfits. The house was immaculate, the living room arranged for dancing and frolicking and real fun, the dining table set for a good four-course meal.

Miss Merline was in her element in the kitchen and music was playing in the background.

"Janice! Come, bring some drinks. The guests are thirsty," Mr. Soares called above the general buzz.

Janice stepped out with glasses of fruit punch. Her high heeled shoes felt uncomfortable under the weight and she felt her head reeling as she walked out in her new dress and apron to serve the guests.

She saw Catalina first. She stood among some young men, her little black dress the picture of sophistication and high fashion. Janice stood and stared, wondering if she should turn back or just drop the tray and faint. She did neither. She faced the crowd who scarcely saw her but saw instead the tray of glasses with fruit punch. Catalina moved away and came towards her. She was chatting to one of the young men as she lifted her right hand to take the drink. She put the drink to her lips and tasted it, still glancing at the young man as she did so. Then she sipped the drink and looked at Janice. Her eyes narrowed to slits and then she broke into a wide malicious smile. She said nothing but turned away and said to the young man, "The drink is nice, try it."

She ignored Janice and continued her conversation.

Janice felt a hatred burn her guts worse than the fires of hell.

Chapter 5

Janice walked through the school gate with her head held high like a giraffe sniffing at tree branches far above. She looked neither left nor right and so ignored Serena when she called from one of the corridors.

Serena shook her head. What was up now? A couple of weeks ago, Janice had a song on her lips and was incredibly happy and carefree. Now she looked like a cold Duchess that nobody dared to touch. Come to think of it, Janice was acting strangely of late. Was she on the verge of a breakdown or something? She had noted that Janice had redoubled her efforts to succeed in the CXC exams almost to the point of madness. Maybe she, Serena, could mention the change to the guidance counselor. She certainly would not like Janice to have a bad jolt just before the exams. It would be tragic. Serena had a little idea of Janice's problems with money even though she had never visited her home or seen Janice's parents. She knew that Janice had a difficult time as did so many others like herself. St. Eustace's was a highbrow school. Serena herself was not highbrow. Her mother was a teacher and her father a policeman. Serena noted that she would speak to the guidance counselor that very afternoon after school. She wanted to help her friend.

Meanwhile, Janice entered the prefects' study and looked at the list of duties for the week. She was on canteen duty. She had to see to it that the students got into queues and bought lunch in an orderly way without too much fuss and pushing around. Janice sighed. She hated canteen duty. It meant that she had to spend her entire lunchtime in the canteen with no thought of going to the library to study for even half an hour or so. It was getting increasingly difficult to study at home with Miss Iris asking her to do things and Miss Merline asking her to iron this, rinse that. Her weekends were full and she had been so tired on Saturday night after the party, that she had not taken up a single book to study. On Sunday, it was cooking and taking care of Miss Iris and helping her mother to clean Miss Iris's room after she had thrown up her dinner on the floor. Janice sighed. Exams were just a few months away and she wanted a distinction in every subject. Not a credit or a pass, but a distinction. It was imperative that she succeeded, not just to console herself and her own hurt, but to be able to lift her head high just as she had done that morning but this time for a reason; she had got all distinctions in all her exams. She wanted a scholarship to begin her course in pharmacy at the university and that meant high grades in everything. She marched out of the prefects' study and went to her classroom with her bag of books bouncing heavily on her back.

She needed to avoid Catalina at all costs. What if anyone knew that her home used to be a one-room in a tenement yard, and that her father was doing time in prison? What if Catalina probed and found out the poverty that she had just come out of? What then? Being the child of a helper was bad enough in the eyes of Janice, but the tenement yard and all she had passed through must not be a part of the secret that was leaked to the other students. She would never live it down. Heaven forbid that it was leaked and became widespread knowledge that she was an inner city girl with no uptown connections beyond that of being a helper for an upper class family. Tears filled Janice's eyes and flowed like a river. Why me, she asked in self-pity, why me?

Why not? a voice inside asked her. Why not you and what is there to make such a fuss about? Many have been through worse times. But Janice would not listen to the inner voice. She was too wrapped up in her own lack of self-esteem and self-hate to see Serena coming towards her with concern marked all over her face.

"Janice," she said. "What happen girl? Why you crying so? Somebody dead for you?"

"No," blubbered Janice.

"Is boyfriend trouble?"

"No."

"You pregnant?"

"No."

"Then is what? Period pains?"

"No. Just leave me alone. I will be alright."

But Serena did not leave her alone. She felt that Janice was going through some kind of depression. Instead, she put her arm around her friend and led her under a tree where they sat on the bench provided. Janice cried her heart out. Serena sat with her, more determined than ever to see the guidance counselor about this. Janice needed help.

After Janice stopped crying, Serena told her to stand and let them both go to the counselor. She was certain that the counselor would help. Janice stood reluctantly but followed Serena back upstairs to the counselor's office. Serena knocked on the door.

"Come in," said Mrs. Wilson. "Come on in."

The two girls entered. Serena addressed Mrs. Wilson.

"Miss I think that Janice needs to talk to somebody. Maybe you can help her. She has been crying and I don't know what the problem is."

"Ok Serena, thank you. You can go. I will speak to Janice."

"Yes Miss," said Serena, lingering a little, looking anxiously at her friend.

"It's ok, you can leave her. I will get to the bottom of this. Don't worry now," said Mrs. Wilson.

Serena left. Janice sat down on the sofa and started to cry again. Mrs. Wilson sat beside her and held her by the shoulders. She allowed her to cry and then she helped her wipe the tears and said, "Now, you want to tell me what the problem is?"

"Miss, you not going to understand," said Janice fearfully.

"Why not try and see if I will understand?"

"Miss... I am so afraid."

"Afraid of what, Janice?"

"Afraid that the students will find out all about me..."

"What is there so bad to discover about you? You are a nice girl. What have you done? Are you pregnant?"

"No Miss."

"You want to tell me? Or you are afraid of me too?" asked Mrs. Wilson.

"No Miss. I am not afraid of you," said Janice. "Miss, my mother poor. She used to wash people clothes to send me to school. Mi father is in prison and now Catalina Nathan know that I work as a helper in the same home where my mother work as a practical nurse to an old lady. Miss, Catalina hates me and she will spread it."

"And what if she spreads it? You think it will hurt you real bad?"

"Yes Miss. I used to live in a tenement yard till a couple months ago. I didn't want anybody to know. Catalina might find out. She hates me, Miss. And she is rich. She don't understand."

Mrs. Wilson looked at Janice as Janice paused and a fresh round of tears came flowing down.

There was silence in the room except for Janice's muffled sobs. Janice wiped her nose after the fresh outburst and awaited the response of the guidance counselor.

"I am going to tell you a story," Mrs. Wilson said, finally speaking.

"Once upon a time there was a little girl who lived in the depths of the country with her mother and five brothers and sisters. Her mother cut stones for the road and sometimes sold sweets at the school gate. Sometimes she sold goods in the market. She came to Kingston on the market truck and slept in Coronation Market some nights. The little girl had to take care of her brothers and sisters as their father had died much earlier from cancer. It was a struggle for the entire family to survive. The two pear trees and the couple of mango trees, and breadfruit and ackee trees and banana plants in the yard, always gave them something to eat during hard times. There was a time when the little girl was ashamed that her mother sold sweets at the school gate, ashamed that she slept in Coronation Market on weekends, ashamed that one of her brothers became a ganja planter to supplement the family's income and when caught, was put in prison. You know who that little girl is?"

"No Miss," Janice said, looking at her with wide open eyes.

"That little girl was me. Me. I was ashamed but at the same time I was happy that my mother worked so hard to help us because she cared so much about us. My mother sacrificed everything for her children as I am sure that your mother is now doing for you. We were ashamed sometimes but we were happy growing up. There were times when I did not even know that we were so poor. Catalina may be rich but she too has problems. Money is not everything. Our history, Janice, is a history of struggle, survival and triumph. Just don't let down your mother. Work hard. Live clean and cherish the love you have for your mother. My mother is dead now. I can't tell her thanks anymore. I wish I could." Her voice trailed away a little as she thought about the past and what had happened to her childhood. Janice sat and watched her and after a while, Janice began to smile.

"Miss, thanks," she said. "I thought that nobody had as big a problem as me."

"Janice we all have our problems. Our duty is to stand up to them and live life the good clean way. We will be alright in the end. Don't worry. Catalina can't hurt you if you see your own strengths. Walk tall. Ok?"

"Yes Miss."

When Janice left Mrs. Wilson's office that morning, she was no longer crying. She felt lighter and much happier. 'Sharing your plight with someone was like sharing an oversized meal', were the counselor's last words to her. She remembered Maas Jonas had always said that to her. He had been her counselor in the inner city. She had often gone to either Maas Jonas or Miss Hillman with her woes, and they had spoken to her and helped her to solve them. Janice realized now just how much she missed them. She missed Miss Clara, the baby, Simone, Charlie and his little sister, and even the standpipe in the yard.

She went to class and handed the teacher a note that the counselor had given her. It asked that she be excused for being late. Miss Myers noted her puffy eyes but said nothing. Janice sat down and turned and smiled at Serena. Serena winked and smiled back at her. By lunchtime, Janice was too deep in English literature and the book, To Kill a Mocking Bird, to care too much about her troubles. She went to her canteen duty and began her job there for the day. Canteen duty was to last for three hours.

The day passed without too much incident after that. That evening Serena joined her on her way to the bus stop and they chatted.

"You ok now?" Serena asked.

"Yah man I am fine. Thanks Serena."

"It's ok. That's what friends are for."

"I know," answered Janice shyly. "One day I will help you too."

"Oh, come on Janice," said Serena.

"No seriously. I want to."

"Here is my bus," said Serena, as a large gray bus came lumbering up the road. The bus stopped and Serena boarded it just as a route taxi came and stopped, and Janice jumped in.

That evening, Janice dutifully ironed all three school uniforms and some shirts for Mr. Soares. As she ironed, she noticed just how few times she really saw the children. After they came in, they went straight to do their homework and then to watch television or to read in the library. Janice realized too that she had scarcely had a chance to look at the books in the library. She was so busy at home. Mr. Soares came in late and went out very early in the mornings and Janice scarcely saw him either. One weekend each month, the whole family packed up and went to the beach house, leaving the servants to relax awhile and take the weekend off.

Janice was glad for those times. She loved to make sure that the living quarters were clean and that she studied really hard on those weekends. She often cooked for all who were left in the house, and together they sat in the kitchen and chatted after the Sunday meal. It was a really relaxing time. Some weeks went by and Janice was back to her old form. Exams were just around the corner, two months away now. It was one of those weekends, a Saturday afternoon when the family was away, that Janice decided to go to the library to find her a book that would assist her with her history essay. She entered the library and noted the almost dead silence that pervaded the place. She found a book after searching among some textbooks on a shelf. Happy to have found it, Janice sat down and began to read. She found the chapter that she needed: Slave Resistance in the West Indies: the Maroons. As she read, she wrote notes in her notebook. Two hours passed. Janice grew weary and fell asleep. Her book dropped to the floor.

When she awoke an hour later, she found the history book on the floor and beside it was a note that had apparently fallen out of the book. She read the note and gasped.

Cornelia, the note said, I will get you some coke from the man down at the store. I know that like me, you are empty without it. Leave the money where you always leave it. Love Catalina.

Janice put the note back inside the book and put the book in its place on the shelf. She almost ran from the room.

"Dear God, help me, help me. Does Mr. Soares know that his daughter is on cocaine and that Catalina is feeding her with it?"

When she went back to her room, she lay on the bed and hid her face in her pillow. What could she do? What should she do now? Janice felt a load on her shoulders that was heavier than an iron coffin. She had to share the problem with her mother.

Oh Lord! Should she show the note to Mr. Soares? Should she confront Cornelia herself?

Where did Catalina get the cocaine? Was she a dealer herself? Janice had heard of students who sold drugs in some schools. Did Catalina take drugs or was she just pretending? What could she, Janice, do now? She had to help Cornelia to get rid of the habit. Mr. Soares had been so good to her so far, that she wanted to save his daughter from certain destruction. She did not know how to do it. As she lay there in the bed in the back room, Janice prayed. As she prayed her mind ran on Miss Clara. She remembered how Miss Clara often sat in her room and read the Bible on Sundays, and how Sundays had been such sacred times to her. Janice felt nostalgia and tears pricked her eyelids. She had to go back and see them one evening after school. But first, she had to tell Rosemary about Cornelia's problem.

Chapter 6

"Mama," said Janice as she folded her clothes to put them away in the chest of drawers. "You know what?"

"Yes, what is it now?" Rosemary was irritable. She was tired.

"I found this letter..."

"Letter? What letter child? You don't know that you mustn't read other people letters?"

"Yes Mama, I know. But it just catch mi eye and I couldn't help but read it."

"Lord have his mercy on us. What so important in the letter?"

"Is a letter from Catalina Nathan to Cornelia."

"Yes, I know that the two of them is friend."

"Catalina and she on cocaine."

"Lawd Jesus Janice. You sure?"

"According to the letter, yes."

"You sure?"

"Yes Mama."

"The poor pickney. Is that girl Catalina you know. She wicked. Lawd poor Mr. Soares and him try so hard with him children. I hope James clean though. I hope Cornelia don't get him into it."

Rosemary looked up from her musing.

"Where is the letter?" she asked.

"I put it back in the book. I was in the library and the letter drop out of the book that I was reading."

Rosemary sat on the bed and put her face in her hands. She seemed distracted and worried. Janice stood next to her, looking worried herself. She did not like to see her mother like this. Rosemary sat there for some time and then looked up at Janice.

"Anyhow Mr. Soares find out him is going to say that is we carry in the cocaine. Janice you have to get that letter as evidence. We come from poor people place. We need money, Mr. Soares will fire me. Him will say that is we feeding Cornelia and him will soon find out that she taking it. You mark my words. Cocaine can't hide after a time. It tell on them. Cornelia soon start thief and sell out things from the house. Lawd Jesus take the case. Take it and deal with it for me Lawd. You remember the book?"

"Yes Mama."

"You can't go back to the library now. They come home from the beach house already but as soon you get the chance, get it out. Is the only thing we have to defend we."

"Mama, why you don't tell Miss Iris?"

"I have to go pray Janice. Cause I 'fraid that they going to say that is we bring drugs to the house."

"What we going to do?" asked Janice, fear lining her face like wrinkles.

"If you can get the letter we can show it to Miss Merline and ask her advice. She more used to the family."

"I will try to find the letter tomorrow Mama."

"Try? You better find it. Is we only defence. Lawd the

poor pickney. She going to end up dead before her time. And you know I did a wonder. She sending back her food now and she losing weight. Fourteen years old and so sick with cocaine. What will happen to that poor girl?"

Rosemary had a sleepless night and so did Janice. Janice had to find that letter again and they had to let Miss Merline know what was going on. They had to get Cornelia off the cocaine and to do that, Mr. Soares had to be told. The more Rosemary and Janice muttered to each other that night, the more they realized that Mr. Soares had to be told that Cornelia was now on cocaine so that he could deal with it before it was too late. Together they rolled and tossed in the bed, frightened that this had happened when they felt they were so secure and happy in this place.

Just before midnight, Rosemary said to Janice, "But it might not be a problem for us if we show the letter to Mr. Soares you know. Janice, tomorrow you have to look for it, find it and give it to me. I have to show it to Miss Iris and then Mr. Soares."

Suddenly the problem was not so big after all. It was a problem that they could deal with if they approached it the right way. Janice fell asleep about two o'clock that night and woke with rings under her eyes and a burden on her shoulders.

She had to find an excuse to go to the library that morning before starting out to school.

That morning, she asked Mr. Soares if she could borrow a history book that she saw in the library when she was dusting over the weekend.

"Yes Janice, go ahead," he answered absentmindedly as he read the morning papers. He seemed to have something on his mind.

Janice went into the library and went to the spot where the book was. It was gone. She searched everywhere. It was just not there. It was then she remembered that Cornelia usually did her homework in the library after they came in from the beach house and that the book was one that some schools also used in fourth form. Janice was close to tears. She did not dare search Cornelia's bag where she was sure that the book was being kept to go to school that morning. And anyway, Cornelia had her bag in her bedroom where she was getting dressed. Janice looked around again. No book. No note. She left the room and entered the corridor. Mr. Soares looked up from his papers as she passed the dining room.

"Found it?" he asked.

"No sir," said Janice, trying to disguise the tears in her voice.

"Well, you can ask Cornelia this evening. She probably has it. She has a history project due tomorrow. Maybe she can let you borrow it later on when she has finished with it."

"Yes sir. Thank you sir," said Janice.

Rosemary was washing some underwear for Miss Iris when Janice passed the laundry room on her way to the gate.

"Find it?" she whispered.

"No." Janice shook her head.

"Lawd, have his mercy on us." Rosemary bent her head to her task and scrubbed the soft underwear extra hard.

"Alright Mama. See you. I think she have it in her bag. Mr. Soares say she doing a history project."

"Alright mi love. Keep the faith."

Janice went through the gate and down the road towards the bus stop where she took the route taxi to school. Exams were close now. Just two months away and she had been working extra hard. She wanted to succeed to please not just herself but her mother too. She wanted nothing to disrupt her now and certainly not a job loss for her mother and herself. They had not been able to save enough in the few short months they had been at this new place. It would probably mean going to another tenement yard and paying rent till her mother found a new job. They simply did not have enough money to pay for more than a one-room in an inner city tenement yard. Neither Simon nor Miss Merline would have the problem that they had. Those two had been with the Soares family for years. Rosemary and her daughter were the new kids on the block. They would be the first ones suspected of supplying Cornelia with cocaine. If things began to disappear, they would be the ones suspected of stealing.

Janice arrived at school worn out and disheveled. She could barely concentrate. She got her math problems all wrong and sat puzzled as the teacher of Spanish revised the subjunctive mood with the class.

Frightened at her lack of concentration and her general feeling of despair, she went to the library during lunchtime to try to read and understand some of the concepts that she had not understood that morning. It was impossible. Janice wondered if she was losing her mind and when Serena, seeing her distraction and wondering what was the difficulty now, came up behind her and said, "Janice you alright?" Janice jumped as though out of her skin, wondering if she was hearing voices and getting mentally ill.

Serena sat for a while and chatted with her. She did not question Janice as she knew that Janice was a very private person who needed to keep her problems to herself, but she actually got her friend smiling by cracking a joke about the chemistry teacher and what had happened in the lab that morning.

At the end of the school day, Janice took the route taxi and went home. She knew she needed to sleep before doing her homework, but first she had to press her uniforms and take over from Rosemary for a while so that Rosemary could do some of the chores in the home. Janice wondered if it would ever end, all this work and worry that seemed to encompass her now. As she stepped through the gate, she felt a nagging fear. What was it? Had something happened? Or was something about to happen? She passed the dogs and saw Simon cutting back the bougainvillea plant that hung over the fence. The sun was still shining brightly. It was only 3 o'clock.

"How you do Janice?" asked Simon. There was a smile on his face. If something had happened, Simon did not seem to know of it. Janice greeted him and nodded.

Janice stepped onto the pathway and into the room that she shared with her mother. The room was as immaculate as ever. As she came out after putting down her schoolbag, she saw Miss Merline emerge from the kitchen with a large pot in her hands.

Janice greeted her. She smiled at Janice. "You alright?" she asked.

"Yes mam," answered Janice quickly, too quickly.

"Cause me see you mother look so worried today me a wonder if everything alright," said Miss Merline.

"Never get to sleep till late last night. So much school work and Mama can't sleep with the light in her eye," explained Janice. If something had happened, Miss Merline did not know of it either.

Janice went into the main house and saw Rosemary looking as though she was about to fall from her seat. Miss Iris was eating a papaya slowly and Rosemary was picking out the seeds for her and helping her to spoon the firm flesh into her mouth.

"Come Mama," she said as she took the plate with the fruit from her mother. "You go get some sleep."

Rosemary rose gratefully and looked at Janice with a question in her eyes. Janice shook her head and went to sit beside Miss Iris. Rosemary left the room and Miss Iris ate the papaya eagerly. It was one of her favourite fruits. Later, Janice took the linen napkin from under her chin and helped her into bed. She was soon asleep and Janice went to press her uniform and help Miss Merline in the kitchen with dinner. Rosemary was fast asleep when she entered the room to do homework and catch up on the lost day's work.

Janice was at the dinner table in the kitchen with Miss Merline, Simon and Rosemary, when Mr. Soares came into the room to see them. He had already eaten and Cornelia and James were in the library doing homework.

"Janice," he said quietly. "Come here a moment."

Janice stood and went with him. He walked towards the corridor and into the library.

"When you came in here this morning, did you see a pen set on my desk?" asked Mr. Soares.

"What colour sir?" asked Janice.

"Silver plate. It is a very expensive pen set and it was given to me as a gift by my company last Christmas."

"No sir," replied Janice. "I was only looking for the history book and I did not find it sir."

"That's strange. Cornelia and James, did you borrow it for school?"

"No Daddy," they chorused. Cornelia did not look up. Her face seemed slightly flushed.

"I will have to get to the bottom of this. The pen set was right here on the desk last night when I used it myself. To tell the truth, I have been losing a few things from my room too and money from my wallet. If this continues, I will have to call in the police. I do not tolerate thieves."

"I didn't take it sir," said Janice.

"Ok you may go. I hope it never happens again."

Janice burst into tears and left the room. As she entered the kitchen, her mother looked up at her. So did Miss Merline and Simon.

"I am not a thief. I am not a thief," Janice sobbed as she ran into her room and threw herself down onto the bed. Rosemary entered and held her close. It was not until half an hour later that she was able to cease her sobbing and tell her mother, Simon and Miss Merline what had happened. And so the whole story came pouring out. The letter. The book. The loss of the letter. Catalina and Janice's problems with her at school.

Miss Merline sat with her jaw in her hands while Rosemary sat on the bed and Simon stood in the doorway. They were serious and angry. Simon in particular felt the need for revenge. Revenge for the girl who had put Cornelia on something as cruel as cocaine and started all these new problems.

The divorce had been terrible for the children and Mr. Soares, Janice was made to understand, and now that this was happening it would break Mr. Soares' heart. He would never believe that Cornelia would do this to him, especially if he heard it from the mouth of a servant.

"We have to tell Miss Iris," said Simon. "Maybe she wi believe wi."

"No, she might have get a relapse," said Miss Merline. "Dere must be another way that we can get Mr. Soares to listen to wi." She thought for a moment. "Tell you what, you leave it to me. Me will see what me can do bout that letter. Is me clean the room in the mornings. A history book you say? What the name of the book?"

Janice told her. Miss Merline went to clear the dinner table and wash the dishes and tidy the kitchen for the night, and Simon went to feed the dogs. Janice felt better and so did Rosemary who went to get Miss Iris ready for bed. They had shared the problem and now that it was aired, they felt that something was going to be done about it and they hoped that it would be soon. Still a little tearful and fretful, Janice set about doing her homework and studied her chemistry and English literature with a vengeance. This new development just made her want to succeed even more and go on to university to get a degree in pharmacology. She had to take her mother out of this mess as soon as she could. If she didn't, who would? Janice sighed. University meant money and many years of hard work. How would she do it? But she would. She went to bed and had a better night than the night before and she woke up refreshed. She would clear her name and she would see to it that Catalina got punished and that Cornelia was taken off drugs.

Even though their ages were not far apart, Cornelia had hardly made an effort to be friends with Janice, moving to her bedroom and from there to the library and the dining room after coming in from school. Both the children had cable television in their bedrooms so the family did not watch television together. In fact, Miss Iris saw more of Rosemary and Janice than she did of her own grandchildren.

"No love," she had often said to Rosemary. "No love at all. My grandchildren need love and caring and cause I am so sick I cannot do it. My son is too busy for his own kids. Too busy. That's not how I raised him. And that mother of theirs has not even sent them a postcard since she left. Wretch. No love, no love at all."

The following morning, Janice left early to escape Mr. Soares' eyes and the children's probing looks. She saw Simon cleaning the driveway as she went out to the gate and greeted him with her customary, "Good morning Simon, how you doing?"

Simon leaned on the broom in his hands and looked at her.

"How you doing?" he asked. "Feel any better now?"

"Little bit better now that I tell you and Miss Merline. I only wish that Miss Iris could hear though, maybe she could do something about the problem."

"We nuh want to hurt her. The cancer bad an' we nuh want her get sicker than she is now. Leave it to Miss Merline though, she wi work something out. Maybe she coulda even hint it to Mr. Soares or something. But don't fret yuh hear? Just study. Yuh exams soon start an' yuh work too hard fe fail now," said Simon.

Janice smiled at him. He understood. She saw something of Maas Jonas in this young gardener who wanted to see her succeed even though he was almost illiterate himself; and he had never approached her for sexual favours as some others would have done by now. There was a mutual respect between them and he knew that Janice favoured her books now rather than boyfriends. Boyfriends were for later on. At age sixteen she would chat a bit with boys but without the intention of permanent relationships. Right now, she had her books to think about and that was of greater importance. She was happy that Simon understood and respected that.

"See you," she said to Simon as she walked through the gate and down the road. She caught a route taxi and soon came off at the school gate. She felt quite happy as she left the sidewalk and walked onto the school compound. The schoolyard was teeming with students and the bell for devotion went just as she entered her classroom and put down her schoolbag. She walked into the hall with the rest of the students and took her place with the fifth formers, close to the back row. The sixth formers were behind her as usual. As she stood there, she thought she heard a giggle and someone whispered thief to another sixth former. She wondered who it was and looked behind her. There was Catalina whispering and giggling and pointing at her. So Cornelia must have made a telephone call to Catalina that night and told her of the problems at home. Janice knew that her difficulties at school were going to increase three-fold. For one thing, Catalina was going to make sure that Janice never ever knew of the cocaine deals for fear that she would let on to Mr. Soares just what was happening to Cornelia, and for another, Janice knew that her mother's position was going to be widespread knowledge at school. Janice felt as though she could sink through the floor. She hardly heard what was being said and she did not sing a line of the chorus that was raised at the end of devotion. Perplexed and deathly afraid, she walked back to her classroom wondering what to do to stop the rumours that Catalina was about to spread about her.

In a school where students of wealthy influential parents made up the bulk of the school population, it was difficult for the child of a helper to be accepted. Janice had always felt the pain of being different. When she first arrived, her broad creole had been the subject of mockery and laughter. She had learnt to speak English language the hard way, pronouncing words as her teachers taught her and reading widely to improve her language skills. Now she spoke and wrote English as well as anyone else, just as she spoke creole as well as anyone else did in the environment of the inner city where pure English speakers were sometimes mocked and ridiculed. Janice lived in two worlds and she knew it. It was difficult to exist in both worlds but others had done it and escaped the world of the oppressed to dwell in the world of the affluent or moderately wealthy, and Janice was determined to do that.

From that morning for the rest of the weeks that followed, Janice socialized with girls whose lips tightened when they saw her. She saw averted eyes and heard taunts as she passed by. So acute did the feelings become that she went back to the guidance counselor who had herself heard some of the rumours. Janice poured her heart out as she told the counselor her problems. But she never let on about Catalina's destruction of Cornelia. She had no proof and Miss Merline had searched Cornelia's room and found no letter, even though she had seen the book. Apparently, Cornelia had destroyed the letter fearing discovery by her father.

It was difficult for Janice to face her exams with all these problems before her, but the encouragement of those at home who knew, and the guidance counselor and Serena at school, helped her through those difficult weeks. Many days passed when tears would fill her eyes and she would long for the security of the tenement yard and the little baby smile of Junior as she bathed him and put him to bed. She longed to bathe under the standpipe in nothing but her panties, and she longed to see Miss Jenny have chicken foot soup on a Saturday evening or go to church in her best clothes on a Sunday with her big battered bible under her armpit, and her one old red handbag in her hands. But that world was behind her now. Catalina gained in popularity while Janice suffered. Rosemary often said to her, "Let her be. She will meet her waterloo."

Little did Janice know how close that meeting was for Catalina.

Chapter 7

Life continued with its ups and downs for a couple more days. Conditions became more relaxed at school and Janice continued to see the counselor for help and guidance. Serena was her staunch friend and her teachers encouraged her to study hard in spite of all the difficulties she seemed to be going through. Her grades were better than ever, causing her to remember Miss Hillman saying, "When things get tough, the tough get going." Janice did not allow the murmurs and mocking laughter to prevent her from working hard, and by the time it came along for the students to go off on a week's study leave before exams, Janice was confident that she would succeed.

The Sunday morning before the week's leave was to begin, Janice went to the kitchen to help Miss Merline with breakfast and to start preparing for Sunday dinner. The rice and peas had to be just right and the coconut had to be blended and prepared for the pot. Roast chicken was to be done and also potato salad and vegetables. Janice loved to help Miss Merline prepare Sunday meals.

"So you off school tomorrow," noted Miss Merline as she prepared the peas for the large pot.

"Yes," said Janice as she diced the coconut for blending in the blender.

"Good. Cause I still seeing what I can do about Cornelia. She not looking well and last night she lock up in her room crying. I want to tell Mr. Soares but I 'fraid if him think is one of we feeding her with it. You know how these big rich people stay, them think that poor people will do anything for money, even kill. Every thing happen in this country them blame it on us, the poorer class of people, and some of them rich man them you don't know how them get them money. Some of them who grace the church steps is the biggest druggist roun' town. Nobody investigate them bank account. Is so-so poor man go to prison for quattie."

There was silence in the room for a while and then the blender started crushing the parts of the coconut that Janice had put into it.

"Bwoy I can't afford for Mama to lose the job here now you know Miss Merline. Things hard in Jamaica and jobs like this hard to get. If she did have a visa... but even America tough now. The waiting lines for jobs there long now after the recession, and I want my mother to stay here. In spite of all the crime, Jamaica is still a nice place to live."

"Is our country this. Is mine and your great grandparents make this country. Is our forefathers were the slaves on the plantations. Is them clear the ground. Is we must build it up. Me not running away leave it even though me is just the helper. Me still have hope that me can make it. Have a house of me own one day and have a little something in the bank. But like you, me nah thief," said Miss Merline.

"Miss Merline thank you for believing in me. Is not everybody would believe in a stranger from the ghetto. People believe that every ghetto youth bad. That not one good person live there," said Janice.

"Is country me grow up. But we did poor," said Miss Merline thoughtfully. "Me grow up on bammy and fish, sweet potato and salt mackerel. But my mother could cook so she used to cook in the primary school canteen. My father used to be a labourer and used to work land for people and is two acres of land me grow up on. Rear goat and fowl and have fruit trees around the yard. Plant cassava for the bammy and sweet potato on lease land when him not working for anybody. Could hardly read and write but him did honest. Is him teach me not to thief." Miss Merline wiped her eyes. "Them dead and gone now but them was good people, my mother and father. Good as gold."

"Bwoy me wish me did grow in the country like Mama. She say that life was nice there."

"Country life sweet, but slow. Like when yuh have to walk to parish tank two time a day for water during drought, when yuh tank in yuh back yard empty," said Miss Merline.

"But even that must be sweet. Mama say them used to sing song at the parish tank side when they washing the clothes." Janice's eyes looked longingly at the trees outside as though wishing she was by the water tank.

"And is like everybody is mama and papa and auntie and uncle to the pickney them. Everybody care 'bout them one another those days," said Miss Merline as she strained the coconut milk and poured it into the pot that was bubbling with the red peas and smelling of thyme and hot peppers.

There was silence again except for the sound of the boiling pots simmering on the fire. Janice looked outside at a blooming oleander tree and thought how lovely it would look on a large lawn in the country with the house on top of a hill. She sighed.

Just then, James came into the kitchen. It was unusual to see James enter the kitchen except to take a drink of water from the fridge. He looked frantic with worry.

"Miss Merline you washed my new Nike t-shirt? It didn't need washing. I did not wear it yet."

"No James. It was hanging in your closet. Look in there again," said Miss Merline.

"I look everywhere and I can't find it and I wanted to wear it to Chukka Cove," answered James. He seemed about to burst into tears.

Janice and Miss Merline exchanged looks.

"When yuh miss it? When last yuh see it?" asked Miss Merline.

"Last night," answered James.

"Janice, watch the pot them. Let me go see if I can find it," said Miss Merline as she went with James through the dining room and into the corridor. She entered Cornelia's room. Cornelia was in the library.

Miss Merline went towards a drawer and picked out a parcel. She did not like doing this but she had to in order to protect her fellow workers from false accusations. She had noticed the parcel as she put away some of Cornelia's clothes that morning.

"Open it," she told James.

James tore the paper. Out came the t-shirt and a pair of gold cuff links that belonged to their father.

James looked at her in astonishment. "You made the parcel?" he asked angrily.

"No, your sister did it," answered Miss Merline.

"But why?"

"Don't know. You ask her," said Miss Merline.

"What she doing with my t-shirt?"

"Ask her."

"And Daddy's cuff links. She can't wear that. She is a girl."

James ran through the corridor and into the library. "Cornelia!" he shouted. "Cornelia you better answer!"

"Shhhh..." said Rosemary with her finger to her lips as she tip-toed rapidly through the corridor. "Miss Iris sleeping. Shhhh don't wake her."

James seemed not to hear her. Cornelia had locked the library door with the key. James banged on the door.

"Open it!" he shouted. "Open it or I will call daddy on the phone!"

"Just leave me alone!" shouted Cornelia from inside the library. Her voice was muffled and seemed remote.

"How dare you interfere with my t-shirt?" shouted James.

"Which t-shirt?"

"The Nike t-shirt in this parcel that you had here!"

"Where did you find it?" asked Cornelia as she opened the door.

"In your room, you bloody thief. What were you going to do with it?"

"How do you know that I made the parcel? Why don't you ask the helpers?"

"It was in your room fool, in your drawer. Janice never enters your room."

"Then ask Merline, she cleans my room every day."

Miss Merline stood and listened while the barrage of words seemed to go on and on. It was as though she had known that Cornelia would accuse her of the theft. James, furious as ever, looked at Miss Merline from under his eye lids.

"How did you know what was in the parcel?" he asked turning to her.

"I saw the shirt on her bed and then a little after that I saw the parcel so I figured that was what was in it," answered Miss Merline.

"How long has this been going on?" asked James of Miss Merline who stood as composed as a judge.

"For weeks now. She makes parcels and takes them with her to school in her schoolbag."

"But why? Is that where all dad's things have gone?"

"Ask her," answered Miss Merline.

"Are you saying that I am a thief?" asked Cornelia defiantly.

"No, but I don't know what you do with all the things that you take out of the house, even some of your own best clothes," said Miss Merline quietly.

"We all know that Janice is a thief," said Cornelia, her bottom lip trembling uncontrollably.

"Search Janice's room and then find out what she could do with these things," said Miss Merline.

"She sells them," said Cornelia

" To who?" asked Miss Merline.

"How am I supposed to know? Catalina said that she is gutter bred. She comes from the ghetto," said Cornelia.

"Cornelia, do you have a boyfriend?" asked James, "and what kind of person is he if he takes these things from a girl?"

Cornelia burst into tears and slammed the door in their faces. James began to sing out loud for everyone to hear "Cornelia has a boyfriend. Cornelia has a boyfriend!"

"Shut up your mouth, you wretch!" screamed Cornelia.

"I tell you what Cornelia, you tell me who he is and I will not tell a soul, not even daddy," said James.

"You know something, let me go finish the dinner. You two work it out yourselves," said Miss Merline.

Just then Rosemary came running into the corridor.

"Miss Merline! Quick! Quick! Miss Iris, she not so well," said Rosemary.

"Lord have his mercy. Is not a stroke?" asked Miss Merline as she rushed towards Miss Iris's room.

"See there now Cornelia, you made grandma have a stroke!" James said as he rushed towards the bedroom behind the helpers. He cried out loud when he saw the condition of his grandmother in the wheelchair. She was stiff and weak and she was foaming at the mouth as though she was having a fit.

"Grandma," he said, moving rapidly towards her. "Don't die." James began to cry quietly as he held her hands in his.

Rosemary and Miss Merline lifted her gently onto the bed and Rosemary held her while Merline called the doctor and then called Mr. Soares on his mobile phone. Janice helped Rosemary to soothe Miss Iris and by the time the doctor arrived, she was lying quietly but her face was a bit twisted and she was unable to speak. Mr. Soares came in and sat beside his mother while his lips moved in a silent prayer.

Janice cooked dinner that day while Miss Merline helped Miss Iris by rubbing her feet and hands. Rosemary stayed with them and Simon set the table while Janice dished dinner and served the food on trays to the family.

The doctor said that it was a mild stroke and that she should recover but there was to be no noise, just dead quiet around her. In the confusion, Cornelia and James forgot their differences and the quarrel that they had had. All thoughts focused on Miss Iris and when she looked up and tried to smile at Rosemary, they all felt relieved. Simon washed the dishes and cleaned up the kitchen while Janice went to study. Exams were next week and she could not afford to fail. It was late in the night before Rosemary came in saying that she seemed to have stabilized and that at last she, Rosemary, would get a nap for an hour or so.

"Mama, what was the quarrel about?" asked Janice who had not heard everything in the large house since she had been in the kitchen during the quarrel.

"I don't really know. Seems that Cornelia stole James new Nike t-shirt and James found out," said Rosemary sleepily. She was soon fast asleep.

Janice decided to ask Miss Merline what had happened as apparently it was the cause of Miss Iris' stroke. It was a long time before Janice slept and she tried not to toss and turn so as not to disturb her mother. Finally, she looked out the window and saw the full moon peeping out behind dark clouds. There was light on the horizon and Janice remembered the little proverb about the silver lining. She uttered a silent prayer and went to sleep.

Chapter 8

Miss Iris, with the help of Rosemary, Janice, the doctor and the entire household, recovered slowly. The doctor visited daily that week and the physiotherapist assisted her in movement and speech. In between caregiving, washing, ironing and helping Miss Merline to cook, Janice spent time over her books. She never entered the library again and made sure never to go to any bedroom in the big house except for Miss Iris's bedroom. She really liked the old lady and the feeling was mutual. Rosemary worked so hard that she seemed about to drop, but she wanted Janice to have time to study during the days so she refused to go inside and rest.

On Wednesday of that same week, Miss Merline said to Janice, "Janice, you nuh think that you should take a little change, like go away from this house even for a evening or so. Is a pity you mother country place so far away, St. Elizabeth far. But you need to get away from the books and the sick home for something better for a while. Go to Emancipation Park in New Kingston and walk this evening or to Hope Gardens or somewhere. Your exam is next week. You need a break. Me will help you mother with Miss Iris for the evening."

"Yes Miss Merline. Thanks," said Janice." I think I will go back and visit the people in the yard where I used to live. I long to see Miss Clara and Charlie and Shellie-Ann and everybody down there."

"And you sure that that is where you want to go?"

"Yes Miss Merline. I want to see mi roots again. I live there so long. I want to kiss little Junior and look at the standpipe where I used to bathe. I want to go down the street and see Maas Jonas, and I want to pop into the library and say hi to Miss Hillman."

"Alright mi dear but be careful of gunshot down in those places."

"Yes Miss Merline, I know. I grow up there. At least I know when gunshot will bus like nighttime after six. I won't stay late. What time now? Eleven o'clock. I will get out of there by three o'clock or so."

"Alright mi dear. Go on now. Bathe and fix up yuh self."

Rosemary was happy to have her get a break and so it was that Janice went back to the tenement yard to visit with those who had been her family and friends for so long. She took the bus and travelled as she had been traveling for so long. Past the groups of people on the streets, past the vendors and the newspaper vendors who were out shouting, "Star! Staree! Buy a Star newspaper!"

Past the vehicles that plied the roads with people like herself and finally, down into the slums with the zinc fences that she had so lately despised, which now seemed a haven for her. She came off at her old stop and walked down the lane. The same familiar faces but few seemed to recognize her in her new denim dress and new white sandals. She had the same canerows in her hair though. Rosemary still did them for her and maybe that was why when Maas Jonas

who was in his corner with his newspaper in his hands reading as usual, looked up as though he felt her eyes on him and said, "But wait! Nuh Janice. Janice mi love, how you do?"
"Maas Jonas. Is you? Bwoy. It good to see you. It so good to see you."
"Everything all right? How you mother?"
"She all right man. She fine. Only the lady that she looking after sick again. She had a stroke and she have cancer."
"Oh Lord. That hard. How school though?"
"School all right. Exam is next week. I get the week off to study."
"I hope you studying you know. It crucial."
"Yes Maas Jonas. I still work hard. In spite of everything."
"You sure everything all right?" asked Maas Jonas. He seemed to detect a little worry in her voice.
"Maas Jonas everywhere you go there is trials and tribulations. Is not just here in the inner city. Since I go I don't hear one single gunshot. But there is so much trouble of different kinds."
"Don't I did tell you Janice? My son live in Cherry Gardens. Big shot place. But I would never like to live there. It have it good points and it bad points. You can have too little and you can have too much. Them people who have too much always go on like them can't get enough. Them never satisfy."
"So I going to look for Miss Clara them in the yard," said Janice
"All right mi dear. Go on in. I glad you don't forget us."
"No Maas Jonas. I will never forget you," said Janice, lingering a little. She longed to touch his bald patch at the top of his head.
"All right Janice. Thanks. Miss Clara should be there. Charlie might be on the road. Him get a little job on a goods truck. Shellie-Ann should be in school though."
"Good," said Janice. "I gone. I will see you when I passing back."

Maas Jonas went back to his newspaper which had the lurid headlines of a rape, and Janice went on down the lane and turned into the tenement yard after pushing open the tall zinc-covered gate.

As she walked in, she saw the standpipe running as it always had and she saw the coolie plum tree, now without fruit. She saw the tiny wooden houses and the chickens in the yard, the plastic basin in one corner and clothes on the line in front of the houses. The large red yard was clean. It had been swept that very morning and as she walked, a huge ground lizard ran in front of her. She jumped. She had heard so many horror stories about ground lizards though she had never proven them to be true. People said that they would bite if troubled, but Janice had never seen anyone being bitten by a ground lizard.

She listened as she stood there, wondering how the yard was so empty of people and then she saw Miss Clara coming through her door with baby Junior in her arms. Junior had grown and he now wore a pair of briefs where before, his bottom was always naked. It was Miss Clara's time to jump. Her eyes looked blank and then seemed to focus and she realized who was standing there with a broad smile on her face.

"Janice!" she shouted happily as she put Junior down and ran towards her. "Janice is you? Mi dream you last night and all morning mi mind on you. Janice I so glad to see you. You all right? Praise the Lord!"

Miss Clara hugged Janice, holding her tight against her pendulous breasts. Janice was so happy even though she could hardly breathe.

"So how you do? How you mother? How the work? How the studies? Janice I glad to see you! I thought you was in some kind of trouble. You nuh pregnant or anything? Eh girl?"

JANICE

"No, no Miss Clara. I not pregnant or anything. I on one week's study leave. Exams start next week."

"Then, how the work? The old lady still alive? Everything all right?"

" So far. Miss Clara I had to come back here to see you. I miss everybody so much."

"The uptown life not so nice eh?"

"It have its problems and its good things bout it. But Junior hungry now. See him crying."

"Oh poor baby! Come Junior. Come eat," said Miss Clara, picking him up again. "Come Janice. I have some food. Is curry chicken neck and back. I remember you always like mi cooking and you like you curry no end."

They entered the room and Janice looked around. She saw a large old radio in one corner of the dinette set and there was a small gas stove with a cylinder. The beds had lovely silk-looking spreads, the ones sold on the streets downtown.

"Yes Janice. I see you looking round. Things coming to come. I sell food to the people in the lane now. Is not everybody have time to cook. Roast breadfruit on the coal pot outside and they buy it from me. I go to Coronation Market and get the real Jamaican food and I cook it up."

She dished out the food as she spoke and Junior sat on the bed, looking at her expectantly.

"Simone have a stall in the arcade downtown and she go a foreign go buy things to sell. She doing well and she help me no end. She is like mi daughter. Charlie have a job on a truck. I only hope him stick to it and the teachers them say that Shellie-Ann should pass the GSAT for a good school. I hope that she come like you. Bwoy Janice everything still hard but I can find food to eat and feed everybody now. God good to me."

Janice smiled at her. She was happy. Things were not always bad in the inner city.

"I glad," she said to Miss Clara. "I glad for you. Mama all right. Things can bad uptown too. Them have plenty things but is like things still not all rosy. The work hard. But me and Mama try. We try and they know that we try. Them have money but the children don't seem to be happy all the time. Is now I know that money is not everything. In fact, too much money can cause more problems than poor people have. I wanted to come back to mi roots. To see the standpipe and the coolie plum tree and all of you again."

As Janice took the plate of rice, sweet potato and curry chicken neck and back, she thought of the comfort of uptown as against the pokiness of the small room and dinette set around which she sat to have her meal. There were very few books. The Bible had its prominent place on a table in a corner of the room and she saw a tiny mobile phone in one corner of the same table. So there were changes. There was some advancement here in the ghetto. Janice knew that nobody she knew uptown could handle money as wisely as these folks from which she came. They could "tun them han mek fashion" as the saying goes. It was as though the troubles fell from her shoulders and she felt as if relief had come to her through this visit.

She thought that she would encourage Rosemary to come one weekend when Miss Iris was much better and gone to the north coast with the rest of the family. Miss Clara fed Junior and she ate her meal with a spoon while Janice had hers with a knife and fork.

They chatted a little while longer and then she washed the dishes while Miss Clara put Junior to sleep. She made her way to the library after saying goodbye to Miss Clara and kissing the sleeping Junior on his cheek. She had to see Miss Hillman.

She passed the same boys that she had known sitting on the wall close to the library. They looked like lizards lazing out in the hot sun. It was the month of May and the sun was already blazing hot in the city. She knew that few of them could sign their names let alone read the books in the library. She knew that many would die by the gun or end up in prison cells. She knew that they all had baby mothers who they did not support and children that some of them did not own. As she passed they shouted to her.

"What happen, Janice?"

"You nuh 'ave a baby father yet?"

"You a waste time."

"Come on man. How 'bout me?"

The vendors by the sidewalks still sat there with the baskets of fish which they guarded closely with their legs. In spite of the hope that she had felt at Miss Clara's, she still saw some of the despair and the loose lifestyle for which the area was known. The twinge of depression did not end her feeling of happiness, however. She entered the library passing the few flowers growing at the side of the small building that Miss Hillman had tried so hard to maintain over the years. She entered the room and saw Miss Hillman sitting there where she always sat, in the tiny enclosure with the library cards and the books that had come in for the day. Miss Hillman looked up at her. Her smile was wide and welcoming.

"Janice," she said. "Janice it's so good to see you."

They hugged and they chatted. And then Miss Hillman told her that she would be retiring in a few months time. She would be going to live the last years of her life in the old family home in the countryside in Portland. She wanted to grow vegetables and flowers for sale.

They spoke of Janice's new life and Miss Hillman was happy that she had come back for a visit and had not forgotten them all. Miss Hillman told Janice that Shellie-Ann was a reader just like her and that she had been a role model for the little girl. They parted with a hug.

Janice was close to tears when she left the room and walked towards the bus stop. On her way home, she felt relief mixed with nostalgia and a little despair. It would take years to change the way people lived as their minds were set and it was difficult to change the mindset of a people. It would take years of education and a deliberate effort by people like herself. But she still revered some of the values of the poor. People like Miss Clara who knew how to counsel just by a look and a few words; people like Simone who moved forward in spite of the pressures of life; people like Charlie who had gone to work on a delivery truck and like Maas Jonas who refused to leave his roots, preferring instead to live as he always had, a simple frugal life away from the affluence of the son in Cherry Gardens; and Miss Hillman who had not come from the inner city but had done so much to change the mindset of the people like Janice and was now leaving with a smile but with longing, to grow vegetables and flowers in her old family home in the hills of Portland.

As the bus moved through the city, Janice looked out the window and saw what she had got used to seeing every morning in the past. The buildings, the people, the cars the buses, the handcart men and the goats that wandered on the streets of Kingston like experts. The goats moved among the traffic without a single one getting killed, ate the garbage of the people and drank water from the flowing standpipes like humans did. In spite of the hunger, no one wanted to kill a goat by simply capturing one and butchering it right there. Yet almost everyone loved curried mutton with white rice.

The hustle and bustle and the noise and the sound of pulsating reggae music were everywhere. The asphalt was hot underfoot and the air was full of the smells of a city filled with people. There were women whose earlobes were filled with gold and silver earrings with not just one hole pierced, but several to accommodate the multitude of earrings. There were many women with wigs and hairpieces of varying colours. The young boys who were not in school but who pushed handcarts for a living, moving goods for market folk, wore their pants almost below their buttocks.

There were young children who did not go to school even though there were basic schools catering for their age groups in the area. They ran around, some playing ball, some begging, some simply sitting on the corners looking hungry and deprived. Janice boarded a bus to Half Way Tree and then took a route taxi back to upper Barbican.

Soon she was in Barbican. As she glanced at the watch, she saw that it was three o'clock. She would have to relieve her mother for the afternoon and spend some hours in the night studying for her examinations.

It had been an enlightening afternoon. She felt purged as one who had gone through a rejuvenation of the soul. As she entered the room at the back of the house to change, she was glad to have made the decision to relive her past, if only for an afternoon. Before relieving her mother, she went into the kitchen to tell Miss Merline thanks for helping her make the decision to see her past again through new eyes.

Chapter 9

It was as though going back to her roots caused Janice to refocus and to view the situation at the Soares, as just a stepping stone. There is no life without obstacles, she thought to herself. She had learned that from her peers in the inner city. You simply stepped over them or you went around them, but some people lacked the will to overcome. The 'sufferer' mentality was rampant throughout much of the country, so much so that some people made suffering a profession, blaming everyone from the government down, for their problems.

For the rest of the week she worked with a vengeance, paying attention to the subjects that she needed most to get her into university to do a degree in pharmacology. Rosemary worked with Miss Iris for long hours and even Miss Merline tried not to ask her to iron the children's uniforms or to wash the dish cloths. Simon stopped teasing her, allowing her to step past him into the garden to sit under the almond tree on the bench there, and study without interference. It was a week of relative peace. Miss Iris showed signs of improvement and the doctor was pleased. The physiotherapist was also pleased at her progress. Miss Iris seemed determined to recover and that meant that much of the difficulty was erased by her own indomitable spirit and her will to live.

Janice never entered the library in the house again, preferring to rely on her own books and those that she had borrowed at the school library to see her through. She was glad that she had made her own copious notes as that meant she was familiar with the topics, and that she could recognize and remember the facts that she needed to know. By the following Monday morning, Janice was ready to face the first exam, which was English language.

It was not an easy exam. It took thought and courage to see it through and these, Janice used. By the end of the three-hour exam, Janice knew that she had passed the first paper in English and awaited the second, the next day. She was doing eight CXC subjects and she wanted to succeed in all of them. After all, her mother had worked hard and her employer, Mr. Soares, had helped to pay her exam fees. She could not let them down. Neither could she let down herself. Simon and Miss Merline had gone out of their way to help her and even though Miss Hillman probably would not know the results all the way in Portland, Janice felt the responsibility of thanking all her friends by succeeding in her exams and by going on to university afterwards.

Furrows appeared on her brow whenever she thought of university. The cost was prohibitive, way beyond her mother's means, and the Students' Loan Centre which gave loans to needy students, required someone to act as guarantor. All the people that Janice knew, were too poor to be accepted as guarantors and she could not ask Mr. Soares to assist her again. He had done enough. But Maas Jonas had very often told her, "Let tomorrow take care of itself, live for today", and she shrugged off thoughts of the morrow and redoubled her efforts as she did each paper and came home to a meal, more revision and a cold shower and bed each night.

It was a grueling three weeks of exams but it passed without major incident and by the end of it, Janice felt that she had done her best and that her best was good enough.

On the last Friday in May after her last paper, she came home, lay on the bed and wondered what she was going to do now. Life seemed empty and without purpose yet she was so tired that she could not take up a novel to relieve the boredom. She decided to help her mother and Miss Merline more that summer, and even to extend her help to Simon in the garden while she awaited her results.

It was almost time to say goodbye to an institution in which she had been nurtured, mocked, loved, hated, ridiculed and comforted. She had grown. She had prospered through a multitude of adversities and she had now become a teenager with a mission. Janice wanted to change the world. To remake the mindsets of the people around her, to teach them about herself, her roots and the difficulties that she had faced, and so far, had overcome. She looked at the world with the wide open eyes of the young and knew that she had to do something. Only she had no idea how or when. Could a pharmacist dispensing drugs behind a counter do much to change the prejudices that so confused the world? She did not know. But she was determined to try.

But first, graduation. She had been saving her pocket money for months for this. Mr. Soares had not neglected to give her a small wage and she had saved as much as she could. She needed a graduation dress and she needed to rent a graduation gown for the occasion. She knew that she could not afford the gold graduation ring so she kept that out of her mind. She needed her mother to be at the graduation ceremony so she decided to ask Mr. Soares to let Rosemary off for one evening so that she could see her daughter graduate.

Rosemary had to get a new dress and she had to send her shoes to be repaired. She decided to wear her hair in braids rather the expensive chemical creaming of her hair. Janice, who almost always wore her hair in canerows, could easily braid her mother's hair. Graduation was to take place in the second week of June and the graduating students were excited.

There was the graduation song to be learnt, the march to be practiced and the graduation speeches to be rehearsed. Evening after evening, Janice came home tired. She had to see to it that the new dress fit, so she made trips to the dressmaker that Miss Merline had recommended. She would need a car to get her mother and herself to the school. It was inconceivable that she would go to her graduation exercise in a route taxi. That was just not done. So she had to save to take a hired car to the school that Sunday evening. She wanted to arrive in style in her white dress, her hair in canerows and her hired gown all pressed and immaculate to walk up the walkway to the hall and take her seat among the graduates.

Miss Merline promised to take charge of Miss Iris that evening, and mother and daughter dressed carefully. It was not a competition but they had to look good for the occasion. Just before the car arrived, Miss Iris called Janice and presented her with a corsage and a card. Janice was thrilled. She put the corsage of orchids and ferns onto her dress and marched to the waiting car, her head held high. Her mother hurried after her. Rosemary wore a light blue gown and her made-to-look almost new black pumps.

Simon came out to wish her well, as did Miss Merline. Miss Iris sat in her wheelchair on the front porch and waved at them. Mother and daughter sat in the back. The driver took off down the road and headed to the school. He drove carefully with the windows up so as not to unduly ruffle the occupants. The car was small but clean and well-kept. It was in this Toyota Corolla that the pair of Janice and Rosemary turned up to St Eustace's that evening. They alighted from the vehicle, a little nervous but happy.

Parents and friends took their seats and the teachers gathered at the top of the stairs to cheer the students on before coming in behind them. Up the graduates marched to the music of Bob Marley's One Love. All stood in silence as the procession climbed slowly up the aisle and went to sit in specially designated seats. The entire group in the large hall sang the hymn Now Thank We All Our God and the ceremony proceeded.

The principal made her report, and the class valedictorian gave her speech to much applause from the audience assembled there. Then it was time for prize giving and the handing out of certificates of attendance to all. Janice felt nervous. She had to climb the stairs and take her certificate in front of all these people. She would also have to pose for a photograph while receiving it.

But first the prizewinning. Janice sat and waited. She did not think that she would be among the prize winners so she just watched and waited for the next step in the programme. She looked down and saw her mother in the audience. She looked happy and at ease. She saw Catalina Nathan there too. As a lower sixth former, she would not graduate until next year. Janice had chosen not to go on to sixth form because of the cost and because she did not need sixth form qualifications for the four-year course in pharmacology at the university. Suddenly, she jumped. She heard her name called.

"Janice Williams, for excellence in English language and chemistry."

Janice almost stumbled out of her seat as she walked to the sound of applause. She posed for the camera and took the kiss from her vice principal who was handing out the prizes. Then she made her way back to her seat. She was incredibly happy. She wiped a tear and smiled. She saw her mother in the audience with a handkerchief at her eyes. Those were not tears of sadness, Janice knew. If she had not done it even for herself, she had done it for Rosemary.

Janice received her school leaving certificate and soon the ceremony was over. There was more picture taking and more hugs and promises to keep in touch. Serena was going on to sixth form if she passed her CXCs. Janice hugged her and thanked her for being a friend.

Later in the waiting car, Janice opened her prize. It was a book. A memoir about the Manley family. Janice almost jumped in the car with excitement. She had always wanted to read that book. Now she had a copy of her own. Her very own.

It was then that Rosemary sprang her own surprise. Mr. Soares had said that both of them could take the weekend off and go to south St. Elizabeth. He would hire another nurse for the weekend. Mr. Soares had been concerned about Rosemary's health as she looked run-down and tired. It was Miss Iris who had told him how hard Rosemary worked and how much she needed a holiday away from the city. That was Rosemary's surprise and after a day full of surprises and happiness, Janice faced her bed that night with stars in her eyes.

The following weekend a delighted Rosemary and a happy Janice started off for the countryside. They journeyed downtown to take a minibus to southern St Elizabeth. They would get off at Junction and take a route taxi to the home of Rosemary's parents. For Rosemary, it was to be a weekend of rest and relaxation. She knew that she would have to chat a bit to her parents and brother and other relatives, and that she would have to visit other relatives and friends in the vicinity, but she had not seen her parents since

January when she had taken down her furniture to be stored and she longed for the old homestead.

Janice too, looked forward to the trip. The countryside in which her grandparents lived was a great place to be. Although she had no friends of her own age there, she could always chat to her cousins and grandparents. She loved her grandfather's stories and the way he took care of the animals and the gardens that surrounded the homestead. As a toddler, she used to look among the leaves of the ping wing patch, which was a cactus-like plant, for the eggs and she was so happy when she found one that she would run helter skelter over the red yard to hand the egg to her grandma. Grandma would take it from her and cook it and little Janice, who loved fried eggs, would eat the very egg that she had found.

Janice hoped to go and spend an afternoon in Treasure Beach, just cooling out on the rich black sand and listening to the waves of the sea against the shoreline.

The journey down was swift. The minibus went via the highways, by-passing the major towns and then came to a rest at Junction. The taximen came to the bus as it came to a halt, each calling out their destination. Rosemary and Janice took the Bull Savannah taxi and were away in a short time. Past some large houses of block and steel in front of which stretched fields of melons and thyme and escallion. The banks of the roads were red with bauxite soil and some of the houses had a deep red or green or deep blue paint at the bottom half of the walls, to protect the houses from the red stains from the dirt. All along the road, Janice saw goats tied at the sides of the roads where they ate the grass that grew in large tuffs. They were skillful at avoiding the coming traffic, jumping out of the way with their nimble legs and scurrying up the bank side to be safe.

Janice's grandfather greeted them. He held out his arms and hugged her, then he turned to Rosemary.

JANICE

"So yuh come," he said.

"Yes Papa," she answered.

"Mama inside the kitchen. She making bammies. Come. She a look forward to see you."

"Bammies!" squealed Janice as she took off to go to the outside kitchen.

Grandma's hands were covered in cassava flour from patting the flour down into rings, ready to bake on the flat iron on the woodfire.

"How you do mi child?" she asked, wiping her hands in her large yellow apron. She hugged her granddaughter and without waiting for an answer, she continued.

"So you done do you exam. How was it? And you graduate to! Good! Janice you do all a we and you mother proud. Keep it up mi chile. Is university next nuh?"

"Yes. Thanks Grandma," said Janice.

"Come. Take you bammy. The first one I make was for you. I have some fried pork in the dutch pot. You can have some with it. Take a dish from the rack there so. Good. Now sit and eat. I know that you hungry."

Janice grinned and did as she was told. Just then, Rosemary came in and hugged her mother. Then, she too took her fried pork and her bammies and they ate while Grandma told them of the things going on in the district. Who had died or had got married or had gone overseas to live. Later, Rosemary's brother, John, her sister-in-law and their children came into the kitchen. It was a real family gathering. For a long while they sat there just musing and eating while the fire under the baking iron roared away and Grandma stuck new pieces of wood underneath. Janice's uncle John promised to take them for a spin in his pick-up truck and they decided that Treasure Beach was the place to go. They would get the day's catch and take it home and Grandma could fry some for Rosemary to take back to the city. The trip to Treasure Beach would be the next day.

For the rest of the evening, Rosemary and Janice did the rounds going from house to house greeting people that Rosemary used to know as a child growing up. Janice remembered many of the older faces but the faces of the children were new. Then they returned home to a large meal of curried goat and sweet cassava with vegetables and bammies. Janice's stomach was so full that she felt that she was going to be sick. Nevertheless, she went to bed and slept the sleep of the peaceful, thinking just before she fell asleep how sweet the country smelt and how the thyme in the fields and the guinea grass that lined the ground of the thyme bed to keep in the moisture in that drought stricken place, gave off a sweet scent that pervaded everything, and how the tall oleander trees in the front garden of the house helped to enhance the smell.

Next day, they went to Treasure Beach. They traveled through the rolling countryside downhill, past some large expensive houses and a view that rivaled anywhere in the world. Most of the way down was farming country and the red dirt was good for farming the crops that grew there. The mango trees were full of almost ripe fruit and the people walked with a pride and a stance that showed that they were self-sufficient and proud.

They entered Treasure Beach with Janice sitting in the back of her uncle's pick-up truck with her little cousins, and her mother in front with Uncle John and his wife. They wanted to take a dip in the sea and buy fish to take back home. Janice was used to Treasure Beach, having gone there on her visits to her grandparents since she was a toddler. They passed the famous Jake's Place where some of the world's famous people came to holiday or attend the popular literary festival, and turned into the beach where the fishermen had their boats. There were many people on the beach. The sand was dark with seaweed scattered all over it and pigs wandered among the boats looking for fish gut to eat. Dogs were also everywhere and Janice knew that she had to be careful as Treasure Beach was not safe for non-swimmers like herself.

As Janice listened to the speech of the people, she wondered why the residents of St. Elizabeth spoke with a distinctive drawl. Sometimes her own mother broke into the speech of her childhood.

"Yes Maaama" Rosemary sometimes said when agreeing to something or "Aaata mi nuh know weh dem a say" when she did not quite understand what someone was saying.

The fishermen were a treat to listen to. They sat on the beach in worn out clothes or sat in the canoes selling fish. They looked at peace with themselves as though the sea was the only place they wanted to be and as though the beach was a kind of haven away from the hustle and bustle of the city. Janice loved to listen to their talk, their jokes, and their laughter which was low and muted, not the raw raucous laughter of some of the people in Kingston, the capital city. It was as though they did not want to frighten the fishes away.

There was a sort of laid back attitude to life in Treasure Beach. People walked slowly, and spoke and laughed softly. Crime was almost non-existent and everybody knew everybody else. The camaraderie was great, the love amongst the people wonderful. It was a family that welcomed people like herself.

Yet it was not as though it was a place without its problems. Treasure Beach was notorious for the lack of rain and the roads were badly eroded when the rain did come. People drowned in Treasure Beach if they were not careful about going into the sea and there was the usual antipathy among some families. But in comparison to many other places, Treasure Beach was indeed a treasure.

Janice had no bathing suit so she lay on the sand in her shorts and listened as Rosemary bargained for fish. She shut her eyes and listened to the sounds on the beach: the grunts of the hogs, the occasional bark of a stray dog, the sound of the waves, the hiss of the fish nets as the men pulled them about, the laughter of the people and the occasional squeal of a child as he managed to skip the latest wave to come ashore.

    She was happy. Tonight they would fry the fish and Grandma would bake enough bammies to last a week. Tomorrow Rosemary and herself would be going back to the city and to work. But it was a treat for both of them, this trip to the countryside and this visit to the beach. Tonight she would sleep between the clean white sheets in her grandmother's house. Grandma still starched her sheets and ironed them. And then she would wake up to the sound of the cock crowing and they would get dressed and be off. Her uncle would drop them at Junction and they would get a bus there that would take them to Kingston. But as she lay there, she wondered what would eventually happen to Cornelia, and she could not help wondering how Miss Iris was faring and if Miss Merline was able to cope in the kitchen and the house. The sun was on the decline when Rosemary called her from her reverie. It was time to go.

Chapter 10

The journey to Kingston the following day was uneventful. The minibus was half-full for most of the way, filling up only in May Pen and later in Spanish Town. It was as though the trip to the country had cleansed her mind. She felt refreshed, especially remembering the time she had spent lying on the beach and listening to the sounds of the sea, and the sleep from which she had awakened that morning with the fresh air and the sound of the inevitable cock crowing.

In spite of the cleansing of the spirit, Janice could see the furrow increase on Rosemary's face and she herself felt a sense of foreboding.

"What's going to happen this time?" she wondered softly aloud as the bus made its way past the canefields and the lines of mango trees, and the surrounding mountains that seemed to hover over the flat land.

The driver turned the radio on. It was time for the news. Janice continued to dream as she half-listened to the newscast. Crime, murder, the economy, demonstrations, and then one news item that made her ears perk up a bit.

"The St. Andrew police have announced a major drug bust in the Corporate Area. One prominent St. Andrew businessman has been named as the mastermind behind a large cocaine deal. No names have yet been released to the public but the police maintain that this drug ring has been responsible for many of the crimes related to drugs in the past two years."

Another drug man caught. Janice slipped back into her reverie. It was as though she had taken a simple shower and forgotten about it. All her sixteen years, Janice had been hearing of the problem of drugs so much so that she could not understand a world without the drug problem. It was more common than slipping on a banana skin. By the time the minivan turned into Spanish Town Road on its way to downtown Kingston, Janice had forgotten the newscast.

Janice and Rosemary had to wait awhile to get a route taxi but they were soon on their way back to the Barbican house that had been their home for the last six months or so. Janice could not dismiss the feeling of fear as the car roared up the half empty streets of Kingston. It was a Sunday afternoon and most of Kingston was either at church services or home or at the beach.

Rosemary paid the route taxi so that it would drop them right at the gate with the luggage, which would have been difficult to struggle with up the hill from the main road. As they entered the street to the house, the two felt a twinge of foreboding. Had Miss Iris died over the weekend, Janice wondered? Something had happened, but what?

There was a strange silence about the place. It was eerie almost, like a ghost house after dark. But the sun was shining. Simon was no where to be seen. Mr. Soares' car was not in the garage and Janice wondered what had happened to everybody. Rosemary pushed the gate and they entered the driveway. They walked up the driveway and entered their own room after using the key. Silence everywhere. It was uncanny. It had never been a noisy household, but at least the cable television would have been on at this time in the afternoon if the family was not on the north coast. Where was everybody?

The two women entered their room in bewilderment. It was as though a hurricane had swept silently through and caused the whole house to be empty even though the building was still intact. As they put away their parcels, they heard a slight knock on the door.

"Come," said Rosemary. "Who is it?"

Simon entered with a sheepish look on his face.

"Simon is what happen? Where Miss Merline? Miss Iris all right? Where everybody?"

"The nurse in there with Miss Iris. Miss Iris sleeping now. Cornelia in her room a cry and James lock up in the library. Him don't want anybody disturb him. Him vex like hell!"

"Mr. Soares?"

"Him drive gone from this morning. Me nuh know where him gone. Him just gone since early morning," replied Simon.

"Is what happen?"

"One big blow up last night. Mr. Soares put five thousand dollars in him room and him mark the thousand-dollar note them and only Cornelia and James know where him put it. Miss Merline never go in there cause Mr. Soares lock the door. The key was on the same bunch as him car key. Well the five thousand dollars disappear. Is not me. Is not Miss Merline. You and Janice not here, so is who? Is either Cornelia or James. That happen yesterday morning. Catalina come here yesterday evening and Mr. Soares start to suspect that something wrong cause she and Cornelia lock up in Cornelia room long long. Him go in there and catch Cornelia a snort cocaine with Catalina watching her. Him search Catalina bag and find the five thousand dollars with the mark them on them."

"Lord Jesus take the case! Take the case my Lord!" exclaimed Rosemary.

"James burst out and tell him bout the t-shirt that Cornelia thief from him and him tell him 'bout the gold cuff links. Miss Merline tell him 'bout the letter that Janice did find in the book and Mr. Soares so vex mi think him was going go off him head. The whole neighbourhood hear him a cuss. Bad word, bad word worse than criminal."

"How Miss Iris take it? A she mi a fret bout."

"She take it hard. We a watch fi another stroke. The doctor come and give her a tranquilizer so she a sleep now."

"Then Simon, where Miss Merline?"

"She gone look for a frien'. It too tense in yah man. Too much stress. It a kill we."

"So now him know that is not Janice that is the thief."

"Me say everybody name clear man. Clear like rain water."

"So what 'bout the Catalina gal she? She gone home?"

"Den you never hear the news? Her father supply her with the drugs for her frien' them. She herself never take it. She a one a the sellers fi her father. The big drug bust this weekend. A Mr. Nathan a de big man behind the whole drug ring. Mr. Nathan in prison."

"Thank the Lord. A him me did hear about on bus radio. You remember Mama, on the radio coming up?" asked Janice excitedly.

"Then hear what? Him ask Mr. Soares as him best frien' fi come bail him. A dat deh time you hear bad word cuss. Bad word fly like airplane. Mr. Soares say, 'You? You? You who infiltrate mi home and maim mi pickney fi life? Mi must come bail you? Is what you think mi is? Pappyshow?'"

"Boy mi glad mi miss de drama. Mi nuh think mi coulda take it. Jesus take the case and solve it," said Rosemary.

"Boy, mi glad we name clear. Especially Janice name, cause them did have it all over the place how Janice t'ief," said Simon.

"Boy Simon, mi glad too," said Janice, breaking her silence. But she did not have a smile on her face. "Mi sorry for Cornelia though. She have to get out of that thing. She have fi go rehab centre."

"Mi a tell you man. Is a wicked thing them do. Cornelia just fourteen years old and them hook her pon it just for the cash. A suh money sweet? That you nearly kill you best frien' daughter fi the cash?"

"An' him rich already. Boy some people never satisfy. Is like money is a god to them," said Rosemary as she sat with her face in her hands.

"A money rule these days. To some people God Almighty nuh matter. Is just the bank account," said Simon. "Him a say that Miss Merline shoulda did tell him 'bout the letter. But we a say to him say him woulda never believe since we couldn't find the letter after that. We never have the evidence."

"But now the evidence is there. Clear as daylight. Him never have to question it. Him see it," said Janice.

"Wid him own two eyes," said Simon.

A silence fell over the room. Janice sat on the bed and thought of the troubles she had had with Catalina. Rosemary sat still with her face in her hands and Simon stood at the doorway. In the background, a dog barked and a car roared down the road at high speed. What would happen now? Would the whole family break apart? Would they still have jobs with Mr. Soares? What lay ahead for them in this broken home that they now inhabited?

As they sat there thinking, a call came from the big house. It was the nurse who had been hired for the weekend.

"Simon, you out there?" the nurse asked.

"Yes nurse?" responded Simon.

"The missus asking for Rosemary and Janice. They come back yet?"

"Yes nurse. Rosemary, Miss Iris asking for you and Janice."

Rosemary jumped up and hurried inside, followed by Janice. As they entered Miss Iris's room, she raised her pale face from her pillow. Rosemary hurried to her bedside, alarmed.

"No, don't worry. I soon be gone. I just wanted to talk to you and Janice. Nurse, give us a moment alone in here." Miss Iris spoke with some difficulty.

"Yes Miss Iris," said the nurse and hurried from the room.

Rosemary and Janice looked worried as they stood close to her bedside to listen to what she had to say.

"Rosemary, you are one of the most caring nurses that I have had. I soon be gone but I want you to stay here to take care of my son and the children. But at the same time, I want you to study again. I leave a little money for you and Janice. I want you to become an enrolled nurse. Go study and better yourself. You deserve it. Live right here with Janice and see to it that the children live good lives for me. I see how you bring up your daughter even though you're both from the inner city. My grandchildren are growing up without a mother's love. Please help them. Money is not everything. Family means so much more. I want you to take them in hand and guide them for me."

Miss Iris was speaking with difficulty but she was determined to say what she had to say.

"Janice, where is your father?"

Janice hung her head and confessed. "Him in prison mam."

"I thought so," said Miss Iris, "go and look for him. He is your flesh and blood. You need to see how he's getting on and you need a father figure, even if he is in prison. When last have you seen him?"

"Five years ago mam."

"Janice, he needs you. He needs to see his daughter. Are you an only child for him?"

Rosemary replied, "I don't know mam, him did have so many girlfriends that I can't tell."

"Go and see him Janice. It is important, you hear me?"
"Yes Miss Iris."
"How was your time in the country?" asked Miss Iris.
"It was nice, Miss."
"Good. Now don't worry about me, I will be all right. I am going to another place. A better place. I finish my work here. When I go don't even cry. I am glad to go. I am glad you were my nurse Rosemary. Take care of Janice. I know she will go far. And Rosemary, qualify yourself. Don't let me down. I talked to my son already on him cellular about the both of you. He wants to see me before I go. Just pray for me. That is all I ask. And no tears, you hear me? If you crying, cry for Cornelia, not for me. The poor girl gone astray. Lord help her." With this Miss Iris burst into tears and so did Janice and Rosemary.

The nurse came back into the room and Rosemary and Janice left with tears running down their faces.

"All right, all right," said Simon consolingly. "She in a bad way?"

"Yes," sobbed Janice as she dropped unto the bed and covered her head with the pillow.

"She soon gone. She tell us goodbye," said Rosemary.

For the rest of the afternoon, Rosemary and Janice stayed in their room grief-stricken. They hardly spoke to each other. When Miss Merline came back, she too slipped into tears when she went in to see Miss Iris. There was still no sign of Cornelia or James. But Mr. Soares came in that night and watched his mother die peacefully. That was when the weeping really began and Cornella crept from her room and sobbed uncontrollably. James kept a stoic silence but sorrow was written all over his face.

The entire household ate fried chicken from a fast food restaurant that night as Miss Merline could not cook a meal in her condition. The hearse came and took the body away to the funeral parlour, and friends and relatives poured into the house to share and give their condolences. To Janice it seemed impossible for life to go on after this. Miss Iris was gone, gone from this world, never to be seen again by any of them. It was painful. Mr. Soares was more broken than anyone else in the home, not even his friends could comfort him. He had lost his best friend to prison, his daughter to cocaine and his mother to the grave. Would things ever get back to normal?

The following day, Janice called the prison to ask when was visiting day at the institution. She resolved to do what Miss Iris had told her to do. She would visit her father not just once, but on a continuous basis for he was, after all, her own flesh and blood.

Chapter 11

The days were busy after the death. There was no wake as there would have been in the countryside, but the flow of visitors was overwhelming. The flowers kept coming in and filling the house and Miss Iris's bedroom was soon full of the blooms that she had loved so much. Cornelia and James walked around with long faces. Sometimes Cornelia locked herself in her room and one could hear her sobbing. James had accused her of killing their grandmother as Miss Iris could not bear the thought of having Cornelia as a cocaine addict.

There were other things to been done too now. Cornelia started seeing a psychiatrist. Was she so far gone that she needed to stay in a detoxification unit for a while? Mr. Soares had to look after that concern as well as the concern of burying his mother. Although he did not cry openly, it was as though he was weeping inside. He looked worried and withdrawn. He seemed to have lost himself in the troubles of the times and was unable to escape the quagmire that was pulling him down.

Mr. Nathan had got bailed by someone else and Mr. Soares had decided that this was a friendship that he could do without. Meanwhile, Janice heard that Catalina too had to be taken before the courts and that she had been expelled from school and would not be entering Upper Sixth Form next academic year. Cornelia was not the only person that she had fed with cocaine, several other wealthy girls who had been her friends had also been introduced to cocaine by Catalina. All the odds were against her, so much so that Janice began to pity her and to wonder what would become of this girl who had scorned her and lied about her in so many ways.

Janice wondered too how she could help Cornelia to get back on the right track. She approached Miss Merline for advice.

"Go and talk to her Janice," said Miss Merline. "You can be a role model for that girl. She all mix up. She need somebody like you, somebody near her age. I can't talk to her the same way you could talk to her. You is young people together. Try help her. Maybe she will listen to you more than me and Rosemary or even her father. Poor Mr. Soares too tense up and angry to talk to her. Him will just push her back on the coke."

"All right. I will try Miss Merline. But suppose she say that I am just the daughter of the helper? That me can't help her cause me come from the ghetto?"

"Nuh mind that, just try. We must help we one another. We is all one under the skin and money nuh make the man Janice, is character that make you, just remember what me say. You just try. You is educated, you is not a fool and you attend high school but you know 'bout poor people and you know 'bout rich people. Your experience is wider than she. You can help her if you try."

Janice wondered just how she could approach Cornelia. Cornelia had already called her a thief and did not seem to want to be her friend, but she decided that she would try. Later that week, she saw Cornelia sitting under the almond tree on the lawn trying to read a book. But it was obvious that she was having difficulty concentrating. Janice approached Cornelia who looked up with annoyance.

"Hi Cornelia," said Janice. "How you doing?"

"Just trying to be alone," said Cornelia, "everybody just all over the house since Grandma died."

"They just trying to comfort everybody, we all loved Miss Iris."

"I know," said Cornelia, "especially since she left money for your mother and yourself."

"Mama never asked for it. She was just as surprised as you are."

At this, Cornelia flung the book and burst into tears. "Everybody hates me, everybody. They say I caused Grandma to die. They say I killed her. I hate the human race. I hate everybody. I hate Catalina. I thought she was a friend. But everybody just want money and they don't care about me. They just want money. Daddy doesn't care anymore. He hates me too. He says that I am a thief, that I stole things and that I went on cocaine deliberately to bankrupt him. I want to die too. I want to die too."

"No Cornelia, God not ready for you yet. You have your life ahead of you," said Janice as she sat down beside her.

"Oh Janice, what am I going to do? I need the coke so much now and I have no way of getting it," moaned Cornelia with her face in her hands.

"Stay away from it. It will kill you."

"But how? How? I get cold sweats now, I think I will lose my mind if I don't get some coke. Will you get some for me please?"

"No Cornelia. I cannot get you some coke but I will try to get you over the addiction."

"How?" asked Cornelia.

"By just talking to you and being your friend."

"You want to be my friend even though I helped to kill Grandma? Even though I lied about you, calling you a thief?"

"Yes. I still want to be your friend."

"You will stand by me even when I go to the detox unit?"

"Yes Cornelia. And Mama will help you too. She promised Miss Iris that she would be a mother to you just like how she is a good mother to me."

"Janice, does your mother hug you and talk to you?"

"Yes, all the time."

"My mother never hugged me since I was a baby and Daddy is too busy to care for us. Mummy went away and she never writes to us. It is as though she never cared. Only Grandma cared and now she is gone. I helped to kill her and she loved us so much."

Janice put her arm around her shoulders. She held her close. The two girls sat there while Cornelia sobbed and sobbed. Then she said that she wanted to sleep.

"Come to your room Cornelia. Come get some sleep. It will help you."

Janice held her as they walked towards the house. A little grassquit that was picking at the grass on the lawn flew up and looked at them from the limb of the tree. Janice looked at the bird and smiled. It seemed as though the bird was sympathizing with the family and with Cornelia especially, for he cocked his head to one side and looked at her. Even the birds seem to understand emotions thought Janice as she guided the younger girl through the front door and into the room where she slept. She put her on the bed and pulled the pillow under her head, and pulled the bed sheet over her.

"Okay, go sleep now," said Janice.

"Janice," said Cornelia sleepily, "I am sorry I lied about you and thank you for being a friend."

JANICE

"That's all right Cornelia. I have always wanted to be your friend. Just try to get some sleep now."

Janice sat by her side until she fell asleep. Then she got up slowly and went to the door, closing it quietly behind her. She had made a new friend and she was happy. Now she needed to follow Miss Iris's advice and see her father.

First she needed to sit still and think for a while. How was she going to approach her father whom she had not seen in five years and who had given her mother so much pain during their relationship that she had only been to see him a few times in prison? Janice's father had been so harsh to Rosemary that she had washed her hands of him and was determined never to visit him again. Had he changed so much that Janice would now be able to converse with him on this visit to the prison? She had often heard of criminals who got worse in prison as their hatred for society grew and they were unable to adjust once they came out, so much so that they only ended up back in prison again. But then again, she had also heard of others who had been reformed and had actually gained a skill and a belief in God.

She hoped that it would be the latter. What would she wear? How would she address him? As Daddy as she had in the past before he went to prison? Would he be proud of her? Or would he condemn her as one of those females who had dissed him?

She decided to go on the first visiting day of the week and that morning she got up early, prayed about the encounter, bathed and dressed carefully. She wore a simple dress that her mother had bought for her and she wore her new pair of low-heeled shoes. Then she said goodbye to Rosemary who was busy in the kitchen with Miss Merline as they prepared food for the steady stream of guests that still came to the house, and she walked down the road and took a route taxi downtown. She got a bus to Spanish Town at the bus depot and prayed all the way to the prison. Her mother had told her to buy some fast food and to take some of the latest newspapers to her father. Janice bought the chicken and she had the day's newspapers and some of the previous ones. She stepped from the bus and unto the road in Spanish Town where the prison was located with her heart in her mouth, ready to run back to the place from whence she came.

The guard let her in at the gate after a careful examination and she went up the steps and into the building. She made her request and was told to wait, so she sat down. Minutes later an older man appeared with a guard and at first, Janice did not recognize him. He was greying at the temples and there were lines of pain around his mouth, but his eyes had lost their usual defiance and they were actually smiling at her when he saw who had come to look for him. His daughter Janice who he had not seen for the last five years while he was in prison.

"Janice," he whispered, "Janice is you? You come at last to visit you daddy." He held out his arms to her. She went into them and breathed in his badly washed clothes and his love. She was glad that she had come. He was her flesh and blood. He had fathered her and no matter what he had done, he would still be her father.

"How Rosemary?" he asked her.

"She fine and she is now a practical nurse and she going to study to become an enrolled nurse."

"And how you? You do any exam at the school yet?"

"Yes Daddy, I just finished CXC and I apply to go to university if a pass the exams to study pharmacology."

"Praise the Lord," said her father.

Janice looked at him strangely. She had never heard him speak like that.

"Yes Janice. I get save. And I soon get parole. I learn to play the guitar here in prison and I am part of the prison band. When I get out on parole, I want to form a band and

JANICE

go about and give God the glory. Him put me here for a purpose even though it come the wrong way."

"How come you save Daddy? Who help you?" asked Janice happily.

"The prison chaplain and some of the guards. Prison can teach you all sorts of things. The good and the bad. But you have to choose."

"And you choose the good Daddy. I feel so happy."

"They teach me a little welding so I can get a job when I get parole," her father continued. "I want to start mi life all over again and I want to be a father for you. Even though I know that Rosemary don't want me any more. I is still you daddy."

Janice held out the package with the chicken to him and he took it joyfully. Then she gave him the newspapers and he grabbed them eagerly.

"Now I can share the chicken with mi cell mate them and we can read the newspapers. It hard being locked away here. You hardly know what is going on. Like the world passing you by and you growing older while everybody out there living. But I change. I change. You will come see me again Janice?" His voice was wistful.

"Yes Daddy. I glad to see you. I will come every other week."

"Good. So I can see that I have mi family. Mi big daughter."

The short visit was over and the guard came to take her father away again. She went to him and held him tight. Then she turned and walked away through the door.

Later, back in the house in Barbican, she told Rosemary about the visit and the great change that her father had made. Rosemary sat on the bed, put her face in her two hands and said quietly, "Thank God. Thank God. And I glad you visit him. Is your father. Miss Iris was right. I glad that you visit him and that him see that you still care in spite of everything. Thank God."

Janice knew that her mother no longer loved her father, the man who had given her a daughter, but she also knew that Rosemary wanted to see her have a father's love and care. That she needed to have the love of both her parents in order to be a well-rounded young lady and Janice was glad of this. Like everyone her age, Janice had often longed for a boyfriend, but somehow could not bring herself to trust her life to a young man. She feared relationships with the opposite sex because she always remembered her father's treatment of her mother while she was still young. Twice, her father had taken a gun to her mother's head and threatened to blow her to bits. She feared the paranoia and the fits of jealousy that were needless and now that she was growing up, she realized too that her mother feared relationships with men just as much as she did. Instead, her mother had devoted her life to bringing up her daughter alone without the help of anyone else. Going to an all-girls school did not help Janice and she knew that she needed to change all of this if one day she were to marry and have children. She would try from now on to re-establish a relationship with her father and learn from him as best she could, the ways of men.

The house was now full of relatives who had come from overseas and the countryside to attend Miss Iris's funeral. Rosemary, Miss Merline, Simon and Janice were kept busy with the cooking, washing, ironing and the cleaning of the house. The funeral was to be held at the University Chapel and the burial was to be at Dovecot in St. Catherine.

Everybody went to the chapel that Saturday afternoon and the tears were many that fell during the service which was short and inspiring. James was asked to read a lesson and the eulogy was read by Miss Iris's niece who lived overseas. At the end of the service, the mourners moved out for the journey to Dovecot, all except the servants who had to go back to the house to make sure that the food that

JANICE

was prepared was served on time, right at the arrival of the family and other guests. Janice took off her black dress and donned her apron and when the guests arrived, she felt no fear again of being branded the maid's daughter, neither did she see Catalina whose presence would never again grace that house. It was a proud though sorrowful Janice who served drinks and shared food and carried them willingly among the company as they chatted in muted tones and hung about the house, reluctant to hit the road. The get together lasted a long time into the night and it was two o'clock the next morning before the tired servants finally went to bed after the washing of the dishes and the cleaning of the kitchen.

"So Miss Iris gone to her Lord," said Miss Merline just before they retired that night.

"She gone," said Simon. "No more Miss Iris to praise me for how I keep the garden."

"Nuh worry Simon. Just do you best still. Mr. Soares praise you too and Miss Iris still looking down from heaven on all of us."

"The final curtain and the last journey," said Rosemary as she brushed the tears from her eyes.

"Is the way of all flesh. We come and we go. Like a puff of smoke. Like a rain cloud. Like a passing storm," she continued.

"What are we in this world?" Miss Merline philosophized.

"Going to miss her though," said Simon.

"We all going to miss her. Come, let we go to bed," said Miss Merline. "Tomorrow is another day and we all have to be up early. Some of them going to the airport tomorrow morning. I have to fix breakfast."

"Good night everybody," said Janice, yawning.

"Goodnight, goodnight" echoed everyone as they slipped sleepily towards their respective rooms.

Epilogue

The summer passed by uneventfully with Miss Clara sending a messenger to tell Rosemary and Janice that Shellie-Ann had passed the GSAT for a prominent high school in the upper St. Andrew area. Rosemary was jubilant, another child from the ghetto was coming out and assisting her family to get out of the doldrums that the ghetto represented.

Cornelia spent most of the summer in a detox unit and Rosemary and Janice visited her often to give her the love and support that she needed. Janice, in particular, was influential in helping her to feel the need to kick the cocaine habit and to restart school in September, clean and free from addiction. Mr. Soares was happy to have them there and he too, as Miss Iris had done, encouraged Rosemary to try to become an enrolled nurse. Rosemary applied and was accepted to attend classes for two years at the end of which, if she was successful, she would be qualified as a nurse.

JANICE

James became Janice's friend and she helped him with his homework as he attended summer school. He was still angry with his sister for going on cocaine and for helping, as he put it, to kill his beloved grandmother. The hurt would take time to heal and Rosemary assured Janice that James still loved his sister and time would be the greatest healer of that problem.

Catalina was put in a home for delinquent girls and began a career as a con woman which was to take her in and out of prison at regular intervals for the rest of her life. Her father, the businessman Mr. Nathan, lost his business and his home as they was seized by the government who accused him of money laundering, and he was given a lengthy prison sentence.

Mr. Soares depended on Rosemary for another year to help him with his home and children, then he found a new love and was soon to remarry and add to his family. Rosemary decided that she would try to get a house of her own with the help of the Housing Trust and that Janice would help her with the mortgage payment when she got a job.

Janice was successful in her exams but decided to take a year off study in order to work and help her mother. She got a job as a library assistant at the Kingston Parish Library and enjoyed it immensely. She visited her father every fortnight and was happy to see him paroled after another year in prison. Then she was so proud when he got a job at a metal work shop and she also accompanied him when he played at gospel concerts throughout the island. He went to schools, church meetings and clubs for young people, warning them against the use of the gun and 'badmanship'. Janice was proud to call him her father and the love they shared as father and daughter made up for the years that she was ashamed of him.

Serena remained Janice's staunch friend and the two visited each other's houses during that summer and long afterwards. Serena went to sixth form and then became a medical student.

One evening, while sitting in their new home in Portmore while Janice was in the midst of her four-year course at university, she thought of the years of hardship and the tenement yard that she had once lived in.

"Mama, everything change since those years," she said to Rosemary who was busy crocheting a blouse for Janice's twentieth birthday.

"For the better. For the better," said Rosemary. "It can change but you have to make a move. You have to try and make a move. Is like, if you don't try, you begin to be like stagnant water sitting helpless in a pool."

"Mama, you right. You so right. You make that first move and everything begin to flow like a river."

Rosemary looked at her daughter and smiled. Then she sighed gently with happiness and went back to her crocheting. She longed for the day when she would be crocheting booties for her first grandchild. Deep in her heart, she knew that that day was not so far away.

The two women remained silent for a long while. Janice looked around at the small but compact little house that they had bought. It was far from the city and going to university meant a long journey every day, but it was theirs. Her mother had done exceptionally well at her course and was now a nurse at a hospital. Mr. Soares never forgot them. He called them every now and again to find out how they both were. Miss Merline was still working for Mr. Soares but she too was saving to buy a house for her retirement. Simon moved on to work in Emancipation Park as a gardener and hoped one day to grow and sell plants from his own store.

Life was full of changes. The only thing that was constant was change itself. Who had said that? Janice wondered as she stood to go to her own bedroom. The years from she was sixteen to twenty had almost been a lifetime all on its own.

The obstacles would still be there. The hurts would come. But she was happy and she felt more capable of facing them now than she had ever felt before.

CPSIA information can be obtained
at www.ICGtesting.com
Printed in the USA
BVHW090029220322
631712BV00006B/28